Steel Beauty

Halle Pumas, Book 4

She's everything a big bad wolf could want.

Coping with a devastating injury is hard enough for Belinda "Belle" Campbell. Forced separation from her destined mate while she heals is almost more than she can endure. Until she is strong enough to take up her duties as Luna of the Poconos Wolf Pack, however, the safest place for her is Halle. Now, after months of being alone, she is more than ready to be claimed. But is the pack ready for a Puma Luna?

Rick Lowell has waited long enough to bring Belle home where she belongs. He's aware of the danger, as well—and it isn't long before a bitch with an eye on Belle's position issues a challenge. The only way to put down the threat is for Belle to defeat the usurper in combat.

There's only one problem. Thanks to the pins in her broken hip, Belle can't shift. Without that tactical advantage, it won't be a fair fight. With his new mate's life on the line, Rick is forced to make a decision that will change everything.

That is, if Belle gives him the chance to make it.

Warning: This title contains explicit sex, graphic language, lots of doggie (or is that kitty?) style and some songs Rick will never want to hear again. Ever.

Only in My Dreams

Halle Pumas, Book 5

Delayed gratification has its place. This wouldn't be it.

Gabriel Anderson has accepted a unique position in the shifter world. He's about to become a Hunter, one of the few trained and sanctioned to hunt down the rare rogue shifter dangerous to humans and shifters alike. There's one catch: until his training is complete, he must hold off on marking his mate. No problem...after all, she probably couldn't handle the sexual demands he dreams of making on her.

Her mate's apparent desertion devastates Sarah. And his friendship with another woman threatens the bond they should be sharing and building. Maybe flirting with another man will make him sit up and take notice—and finally win Gabe's heart. It works. Almost too well.

One touch of another man's hand on Sarah's tempting body brings every ounce of Gabe's possessiveness roaring to the surface. He wastes no time making his erotic dreams of dominating her a reality—whether she's ready for it or not.

If she's not, the only place he'll ever have her is in his dreams...

Warning: This title contains graphic language, explicit sex, deep blue eyes and spanking. The author is not responsible for any tall, dark and handsome men who slip into your dreams.

Look for these titles by
Dana Marie Bell

Now Available:

Halle Pumas Series
The Wallflower (Book 1)
Sweet Dreams (Book 2)
Cat of a Different Color (Book 3)
Steel Beauty (Book 4)
Only in My Dreams (Book 5)

Halle Shifters Series
Bear Necessities (Book 1)

True Destiny Series
Very Much Alive (Book 1)

Gray Court Series
Dare to Believe

Print Anthologies
Hunting Love
Mating Games

Coming Soon:

True Destiny Series
Eye of the Beholder (Book 2)

Animal Attraction

Dana Marie Bell

A Samhain Publishing, Ltd. publication.

Samhain Publishing, Ltd.
577 Mulberry Street, Suite 1520
Macon, GA 31201
www.samhainpublishing.com

Animal Attraction
Print ISBN: 978-1-60504-810-9
Steel Beauty Copyright © 2010 by Dana Marie Bell
Only in My Dreams Copyright © 2010 by Dana Marie Bell

Cover by Mandy Roth

Steel Beauty, ISBN 978-1-60504-498-9
First Samhain Publishing, Ltd. electronic publication: April 2009
Only in My Dreams, ISBN 978-1-60504-826-0
First Samhain Publishing, Ltd. electronic publication: November 2009
First Samhain Publishing, Ltd. print publication: September 2010

Contents

Steel Beauty

Dedication

To Mom, who thinks, even after seventeen years, that Dusty and I are nauseatingly sweet together. It's not like we make goo-goo eyes at each other just to watch her gag or anything. We aren't *that* devious. Really. No matter how funny it is.

To Dad, who will probably start calling on Dusty again to fix his Diablo II game now that his live-in tech support is heading off to college. Remember, don't let my sister touch it lest you have to restart your level 60 paladin *again*. How many times would that make, anyway?

To Memom, who tells my mother to stop gagging every time Dusty and I make goo-goo eyes at each other. She thinks it just encourages us.

To my brother, for helping me think up ways to torture Rick at a certain Pack meeting.

To Dusty, who has decided that since I've named his laptop "Bertha, aka the Other Woman", my laptop needs a name. Last I heard he was muttering "Sven, maybe?"

And to Crystal Dee, who came up with the name Steel Beauty. May I say you rock?

Prologue

November

"No *fucking* way." Rick stared at Max Cannon, the Halle Puma Alpha, and wondered what his head would look like rolling down the driveway. "My mate goes home with me."

"How are the Wolves going to react to an injured, non-Wolf Luna? Think, Rick! Not only is she injured, she's Puma. And until you can fully claim her, she's Pride. *My* Pride." Rick watched Max cross his arms over his chest. He wanted to rip them off and beat him over the head with them.

He'd had a thoroughly rotten day. He'd been shot, killed a rogue, found his mate, found out his mate was *hurt*, and now had to deal with a territorial cat intent on sending him on his way. "She comes home with me."

Max sighed and rubbed his forehead. "Look, Rick, I know how I would feel if this were Emma."

Rick nodded shortly. The big cat *would* understand, somewhat.

"But, and this is a big but, Belinda hasn't had the easiest time of it in the last couple of weeks. You're new to your position, as well. You need to solidify your Pack and prepare them for what they're going to have to deal with when Belinda gets there. You'll also have to prepare Belinda."

"Belle."

Rick looked at the pale mate of the Puma Marshall, Sheri Montgomery, the one who'd been the cause of Rick coming down to Halle in the first place. "Belle?" Who was this Belle, and what did she have to do with Belinda?

Sheri shot a look at Simon, who winced. Rick's eyes narrowed at the guilty flush on the Beta's face and wondered what the man was hiding. Sheri turned back to Rick with a grimace. "Belinda is who she was when she was friends with Livia, the mask she wore to fit into Livia's social set. Belle is who she *really* is."

Simon nodded. "And that's something else that needs to be dealt with."

Rick sighed and sunk down onto Max's leather sofa. The Alpha had dragged him, literally, out of Adrian's house, shoved him in his Durango, and carried him off. It hadn't taken long for the rest of the Pride's inner core to show up. Only the fact that his own Marshall hadn't been worried for him had kept him from biting some cat ass. "You are going to explain all of this shit, right?"

Emma spoke up. "I'll try. Okay, roughly a month ago Max marked me as his and claimed me as his Curana." Rick nodded. Curana was Puma equivalent of Luna, the Alpha female of a Pack, or in Emma's case, a Pride. "He gave me the Curana's ring, and I wore it to the annual Halle masquerade. When Livia realized Max had mated me, she freaked out. She attacked Becky, Simon's mate, while Becky was still human."

Ouch. That explained why the woman had been Outcast. An unprovoked attack on a human? This Livia person was lucky Max or Simon hadn't ripped her throat out. That's what Rick would have done. "What does this have to do with Belle?"

Emma shrugged. "Belle and Livia were best friends, and it

was well known Belle wanted to mate with Simon."

Rick stiffened. *Mate with Simon?* Now he understood some of why the Beta had looked guilty.

Emma continued the story, leaning against Max with a sigh. "Because Livia attacked Becky, and Belinda wasn't anywhere near the party at the time it happened, most of the Pride assumed she'd helped Livia in some way or another. Hell, even we assumed it at first."

Rick clenched his jaw against his immediate response. He didn't know Belle well enough to know if she was capable of such a thing, despite every single one of his instincts screaming that she wasn't. "What happened next?"

"Livia was Outcast, and Belle..."

Emma looked up at Max, but it was Simon who answered. "Belle proved herself to us. She helped save Becky when Becky collapsed at work, and she sacrificed herself to save Sheri from a psychotic stalker." Simon shook his head. "I never thought Belle had it in her to do that, but she proved me wrong."

"She proved all of us wrong." Max snuggled Emma close, a frown on his face. "But we've had a difficult time getting the rest of the Pride to see that, despite everything she's done. In essence, they've shunned her. She's lost her job, almost lost her apartment, and even with her injury we had a hard time getting volunteers to protect her when she needed it."

Rick bit back a growl. The danger was past, and they *had* figured out how to protect his mate in the end. But the fallout on Belle had been, in Rick's mind, totally unwarranted. Just because her ex-best friend had been a psychotic bitch didn't mean Belle should be held responsible for the other woman's actions. He couldn't wait to get her away from the self-righteous assholes who were making her life a misery.

He stood, ready to walk out Max's front door, put his

female in his car, and take off for home.

"Rick." Becky stood, ignoring Simon's outstretched hand. "I'm probably one of the last people Belinda would expect to stand up for her right now, but I have to say, she's had a horrible time of it. Don't make it worse for her."

Max blocked his path to the front door. "Are there any doctors up by you who can handle an injured shifter? Any who can deal with the physical therapy she's going to need?"

Rick growled.

Max, the smug bastard, smiled. "Are you willing to move down here for the next few months? No? Then go home. Let her heal. Then, when she's ready, come and take her."

"Take her home."

"What?" Max turned to his little dark-haired mate.

"Take her *home*. You said take her."

Max gave her a puzzled frown. "Well, that too."

Rick snorted, amused for the first time that day, as Emma rolled her eyes at Max.

Max put his hand on Rick's shoulder, squeezing reassuringly. "I give you my word that no harm will come to your mate while she is under my protection."

The formal vow, accompanied by a flash of Max's power, reassured him. Looking around, he saw the determination on the faces of the rulers of the Halle Pride, and knew he'd lost this round.

He accepted Max's oath, and the separation that would accompany his decision, with a great deal of reluctance.

But there was no way in hell he was going to stay completely out of his mate's life for the next few months. He might not have her by his side, but he'd be damned if he didn't have *some* piece of her.

December

Belle picked up the little hand-held computer Rick had sent her and smiled. She'd only been out of the hospital for a little over a month, but he text-messaged or called every single day without fail. He'd even set up the chat program for her. She'd laughed when she saw the handles he'd given them both.

BgBdWlf837: *How's my Luna today?*

She started typing on the miniscule keyboard. The concentration helped with the pain, sometimes.

BellaLuna1345: *So-so. Therapy was a bitch. No pun intended. I think my therapist was trained personally by the Marquis de Sade in a previous life. You?*

BgBdWlf837: *Work work work.*

Something he very rarely discussed. One of these days she was going to nail his ass down and find out what he did for a living.

BgBdWlf837: *You get my Christmas present?*

She smiled as she thought of the present he'd sent. A beautiful aqua silk scarf, a pair of diamond earrings, and a thin gold chain had been in the exquisitely wrapped present. Knowing men the way she did, she wondered who he had buy the gifts, or if he'd actually bought them himself.

BellaLuna1345: *Yes. Beautiful. Thanks. You get mine?*

She'd sent him a watch. On the face was a howling wolf. She'd had it custom made by a friend of hers, who'd done the work for cost or she'd never have been able to afford it.

BgBdWlf837: *Yes! Love it! Wearing it now.*

That made her grin, even if he was lying through his teeth.

BgBdWlf837: *Let me know if I need to come down there and rip the gonads off your PT, k? And keep that pussy Beta away from you.*

Belle rolled her eyes. He had a real thing against Simon. She wondered who'd told him about her past relationship with the Pride's Beta.

BellaLuna1345: *Down, boy. Sit. Good dog. Goooood dog.*

BgBdWlf837: *ROFL*

BgBdWlf837: *Merry Christmas, my Luna.*

She couldn't help the big smile. Just seeing his name brightened her day in a way she couldn't explain. Those times when they actually spoke on the phone were the best, though. Then she could hear that deep, rough voice soothing the aches and pains of not just her injury, but her near-shunning.

BellaLuna1345: *Merry Christmas, Fido.*

Not that she would let *him* know that, off course.

He might be her mate, but she could still play hard-to-get.

January

"Wow, you're cranky today." Belle put the phone between her ear and shoulder and scratched blissfully at her arm. The cast had finally come off and she could reach that damn spot that had been bothering her for eight long weeks.

"What makes you say that?"

"Oh, I dunno. The fact that you growled at me, maybe?"

"Oh. That."

"Simon is mated, Rick. He's also my Beta. I have to talk to him sometimes."

"You may have to talk to him, but I don't have to like it."

"Really? Huh." His chuckle was music to her ears. Her gasp of pain as she shifted in her chair, apparently, was not music to his ears. "Don't growl at me, there's nothing I can do about it. Besides, you're the one who agreed to go back north until the doctor releases me for Lunatic duty."

"Belle."

She sighed as the pain subsided. It was so tempting to reach for the morphine when the pain got this bad, but she wouldn't. Jamie was right; she'd become too dependent on it. They'd mutually decided she should go on Ibuprofen instead, counting on her Puma metabolism to get the drug out of her system as quickly as possible.

The night she went off the morphine she'd chosen to text

Rick first, not wanting him to hear the withdrawals she was going through. She kept it short, merely telling him she was having a bad day and she'd speak to him the next night. He'd responded, but he hadn't sounded happy. The next night her phone rang before the physical therapist was even done seeing her. That had been two weeks ago.

"I'm fine, Rick. The cast on my arm came off today."

"Good!"

"Yeah, I can finally scratch."

"And we all know how much cats like to scratch?"

"Very funny, Fido. Har har. Peed on any hydrants lately?"

"In this weather? Are you nuts? I'd be glued to the damn thing until the spring thaw."

She laughed out loud, the first one in over a week.

"Now that is the sweetest sound."

That rough, rich voice slid through her, speeding up her heart rate. And from the look of her no-longer-red nail polish her eyes had turned gold. *There go my panties, getting all wet again. How does the man do that when I'm ready to rip my leg off from the pain?*

She heard the front door to her small apartment open. Turning, she saw Sarah come in, a smile on her wind-kissed cheeks. "Sarah's here. Gotta run."

"Pizza and poker night?"

"Yup. I'll tell Adrian and *Simon* you said hi."

He was *still* grumbling when she hung up.

Chapter One

February

"You're coming home. Three Wolves will be there in the morning to pack your belongings. Your landlady has been informed that your lease will not be renewed, and your medical records have been forwarded to the Pack doctor. Ben and I will pick you up at the end of the week."

Belle pulled the receiver away from her ear and stared at it. Then she banged it as hard as she could four or five times against the bottom of her stainless steel frying pan.

"Damn it, woman, don't *do* that!"

She put the handset back to her ear. "I'm sorry. Did you want to ask me a question?"

He growled. Her Wolf was grumpy tonight. "I need you home."

She sniffed, secretly pleased he'd said that, but not willing to admit it. "I am home."

He inhaled noisily. "*Belle.*"

"My name is Belinda." She waited for the explosion, sure it was coming.

"Don't meet the Wolves with a gun, Belle. They have orders to take it from you."

Oh, poo. There go my shopping plans for tomorrow. "I would never do that, Rick."

She loved it when his teeth ground together. He did it the most when she pulled out her "airhead" routine. His long-suffering sigh was music to her ears. "Come home to me, Belle."

Damn. That sexy growl he got when he called her Belle made her panties wet. *The big dope.* Just for that she decided she'd played enough. "I have a few more things to take care of before I head into Winter Wonderland." She picked up the orange and started slicing it, holding her phone between her shoulder and her ear. *For instance, I need to get a Bluetooth or something.* Money had been awfully tight since she'd been fired from Noah's, and it was about to get tighter. Her medical bills were piling up. Unless Richard was independently wealthy, she'd need to find a job ASAP.

She heard the rustling of sheets. She could just picture that big body of his leaning against a wooden headboard, the cotton pooled around his groin, his chest naked and lightly furred, just like she liked her men.

Make that man. Simon had been her only, until his mating with Becky. Belle was over it, but the first month had been rough, dealing with her broken heart, a broken hip, a broken arm, *and* a new, unclaimed mate. Thank God she and Becky had overcome their differences. She now counted Simon and Becky among her few friends.

"What sort of things, my Luna?"

He used the term Luna the way other men used "sweetheart" or "honey", growling it in that sexy as hell voice of his. Goose bumps shivered up and down her arms. "Just...things." She laughed at his low growl. "*Girl* things, like shopping and haircuts."

"Go get pampered then, Belle." She almost sighed dreamily over the rough timber of his voice. Of course, he had to go and ruin it. "Just remember: no one pets you but me."

She rolled her eyes. "No problem, *Dick*."

He chuckled, sending a flood of heat to pool in her belly. "Good night, Belle. Sweet dreams."

He didn't wait for her reply, simply disconnecting, leaving her feeling empty. "Good night, Rick." She set the phone back in its charger, put the orange slices on the plate and headed for her bedroom, hoping he didn't find out that her special One-Fruit Fruit Salad had been dinner for the past three nights. Mr. Overprotective would have a hissy fit of epic proportions if he did.

I'd probably find a bunch of Wolves on my doorstep with doggie bags. She snickered as she settled in for the night, her water and orange on the nightstand and soothing music playing on her portable stereo. She wished, not for the first time, that Rick were there to share it with her.

"You're joking, right?" Belle looked over at her Curana, Emma Carter, who would be Emma Cannon in two months' time. Emma was staring up at the spa's sign, a look of anticipation on her face. Becky, on the other hand, looked just as dubious as Belinda felt, but for different reasons.

"Emma, are you sure about this?" Becky pushed her long, curly hair out of her face, holding it back in the cold February winds. She frowned at Emma. "Half the stuff they do here, we can do at home."

"First off, I'm not touching your feet." Emma laughed when Becky stuck her tongue out at her. "Second, trust me! What's a better mating gift than a day at the spa?" Emma grinned at the two of them. From the look of things she was eagerly anticipating the coming wraps, lotions and facials. Becky still looked like she was going to a torture chamber.

Belle, on the other hand, was feeling a little ambivalent. She hadn't been to the spa, one of her favorite relaxation spots, in months. Not since the incident with Livia. The members of the Pride, despite Emma, Becky, and Sheri's support, were still very much of the opinion that Belle had been in cahoots with her ex-best friend. So on one hand, she was looking forward to a little pampering. On the other hand...

Marie Howard stepped out of the spa, a breezy, relaxed smile on her face. It froze for just a second before sharpening. "Hello, Emma. Becky." Those sharp brown eyes turned to Belle and all the warmth drained out. "Belinda."

Hypocrite. Marie had been a friend of Livia's too. She just didn't bear the stigma of *best* friend. She smiled her toothiest human smile. "Marie."

Marie turned back to Emma. "Are you and Becky planning on enjoying a day at the spa?"

Either Marie was stupider than Belle thought, or she just didn't feel the chill in the air as Emma stared at her. "The *three* of us are planning on spending the day here." She smiled, her teeth a little sharper than normal. "After all, tomorrow Belinda leaves for the Poconos and her mating with Richard."

Belle smiled sweetly at her ex-friend. "That's right. One more day and you'll only have to deal with me one more time."

"One more time?"

"Belinda has agreed to be one of my bridesmaids."

Shock and, yes, hurt, briefly flashed across Marie's face. Belle still wasn't sure what had made her say yes to Emma's request, but it had been worth it to see the excitement in Emma's eyes. The Alpha and Curana had booked a fairy-tale wedding in Disney World. How Max had managed to swing that in such a short time when the usual waiting period was nine months, Belle had no clue, but he'd managed it, and Emma was ecstatic over it.

Marie's expression was frozen as she nodded curtly. "Good luck, Belinda."

"Thank you." *I'll need it.*

"I'll see you in April, then."

Marie turned to go without another word. Belle stepped forward, leaning heavily on her cane as she followed her Curana and Beta into the salon.

"I'm telling you, Sheri, those women hate me." Belle sighed over her Coke, wincing as she tried to shift her legs and rub the irritation at the juncture of her thighs. The pain that shot through her hip made her hiss.

At least I can move my legs now without wanting to chop them off. Those first few weeks after the surgery had been horrendously painful. Thank God Sheri and Sarah had been willing to be with her during that time. She didn't know *what* she would have done if it hadn't been for them. The fact that Richard had allowed himself to be forced back to his Pack until she was well enough to deal with her new position had caused some serious friction between them in the beginning, even if she could understand why. At least Rick called daily, whether she could talk to him or not. It helped ease the sting of his not being there. And if he had been there, the big dope probably would have decked the physical therapist more than once by now, probably landing in jail or in the middle of a lawsuit.

Okay, maybe Max had the right idea, sending him away. Rick was overprotective on the phone. In person, he would have smothered her. She only hoped he'd gotten some of it out of his system by now.

If not, there was always the pepper spray.

"They do not hate you, Belle. I mean, they took you to a lovely day at the spa." The pale woman sighed, resting one alabaster cheek against an equally white hand. "They never offered to take *me* to a day at the spa."

Belle leaned across the table and held two fingers up to her new best friend. Her relationship with Sheri and her other friend Sarah was one of the few good things to come out of the fiasco of the last few months. "I have two words for you: Full. Brazilian."

Sheri sputtered, laughing.

"Oh, sure. Laugh. Some sick sadist slaps boiling wax on your nether regions, sops it up with a strip of cloth, and then just *rips* it off without a care in the world. And while you're lying there, screaming in pain and threatening their lives, the sadist takes out the tweezers to 'clean you up' while they tell you to suck it up and take it like a woman."

"They did not!"

"Oh, no, the girls torturing me didn't say it. My Curana and her Beta said it while they sipped fruity drinks and got their nails done." Belinda shook her head, trying not to squirm too much.

"Look on the bright side. Think about what they'd do to someone they *don't* like."

The women exchanged a look, well aware that Belle could easily have been one of those women on the bad side of the Curana and her Beta.

"Belle? Sheri? I'm not late, am I?"

Both Belle and Sheri smiled at the sound of that soft, sweet voice. Sarah Parker joined them at the booth, settling her purse between her feet as she pushed her bobbed brown hair behind her ears. "I'm late, aren't I?"

"You're not late, Sare-Bear." Belle grinned as Sarah made a face at the nickname she'd been stuck with for years.

Sarah pointed an accusing finger at Belle. "You are so totally lying, but I'll let you get away with it *this* time." She grinned. "And don't think you can intimidate me, missy." She struck a pose, nose in the air. "*I* am a High School Guidance Counselor. I face much scarier things than you every day."

"Amen," Sheri muttered, toasting Sarah with her diet Coke.

"Ditto." Belle raised her own glass, pleased when Sarah's and Sheri's clinked loudly against hers. No matter how much Becky and Emma did their best to draw her in, there was too much emotional baggage for them to be best friends. In these two women, women she wouldn't have given the time of day once, she'd found comfort and a deep friendship she hadn't known was possible. Both of them accepted her for herself, not the false persona she'd shown the world for so long under Livia's influence.

Sarah had been one of the only females willing to sit with her during her stay in the hospital, when Sheri's brutal ex-boyfriend had been stalking her. Belle had broken her hip saving Sheri from being run down by a car, a fact that had earned her Adrian Giordano's undying devotion. In fact, if Marie had tried to pull that cold as ice shit around the Marshall, she would have been in for a very rough time of it indeed.

"So, how's Adrian?" Sarah grinned at Sheri, but Belle wasn't fooled. Sarah had a serious crush on Adrian's Second, Gabe Anderson. Too bad the man completely ignored her whenever they met. Belle knew that Gabe's attitude was slowly beginning to wear away at Sarah's cheerful façade.

"Fabulous." Sheri drawled, fanning herself with her hand. She leaned in, waiting for the other women to join her. "I got him to agree to moonlight skinny dipping once the weather warms up."

"Oh, you naughty girl, you." Sarah reached into her voluminous purse and pulled out a notebook and pen, all without looking. She opened it with an evil grin. "Give me dates and times, so I can set up the hidden camera."

Sheri cocked one eyebrow. "You are *not* filming my mate's naked butt."

"What about his naked—"

"No."

"Damn. Foiled again."

Belle grinned as Sheri snickered.

"Hey, Belle!"

Here we go again. She hid her grin by taking a sip of soda. "Hey, Frank!"

"What do you call a circle of blondes?"

She winked at Sarah and Sheri. "A dope ring."

The entire diner erupted into laughter.

Belinda smiled at Chloe, Frank's new waitress, as the girl set down Belle's burger and fries. Two similar plates went in front of the other women.

"Thanks, Chloe."

"No problem, Belle." Chloe leaned over to whisper in her ear. "Congratulations on your mating, by the way." She winked and sauntered off, much to the satisfaction of several of the male patrons. A few of them even leaned out of their booths to watch her ass as it sashayed over to the soda fountain. Her bright red ponytail bounced merrily between her shoulder blades.

Belle's mouth hung open in shock. Chloe wasn't Puma; how the *hell* did she know about Rick? She sniffed, catching a whiff of something elusive. Something definitely shifter, but whatever breed the girl was she'd never smelled it before.

"Belle?"

She turned, snapping her mouth shut and trying desperately to school her features. "Hmm?" She picked up her burger and took a bite, savoring the flavor of the meat. Frank made the best burgers she'd ever been privileged to taste.

Soft fingers touched the back of her hand. "Everything is going to be fine. I promise you that." Sarah's eyes had that far away look they sometimes got.

She's probably daydreaming about Gabe. Admittedly, if Rick wasn't such a hunk, she might be tempted to daydream about the black-haired, blue-eyed sheriff herself.

Peace flowed over her, as it always did when she was with her friends. She just wished she could pack them up and take them with her. She had the feeling she was going to need them.

Sarah leaned down and began scribbling something in her notebook, ignoring both her burger and the looks she was receiving. Everyone indulged Sarah in her eccentricities. She was just so sweet to everyone that they couldn't help it.

Suddenly ravenous, Belle devoured her burger. She couldn't wait for tomorrow. She'd get to see her mate for the first time in months.

And if he played his cards right, she'd mark him the moment she saw him.

Richard Lowell scowled at his Beta, David Maldonado, and his Marshall, Ben Malone. The only one who wasn't falling under his eye was his Omega; he hadn't informed her yet of her status. Until she recognized what she was, it would be a useless endeavor, ending only in more pain and degradation for her.

"Let me rephrase that. I need you to pick up Belinda for me *without arguing.*"

Ben had a faint frown on his face, while Dave was openly scowling. "Why aren't you going to get your mate yourself?"

Richard sighed and leaned back against his sturdy oak desk. What part of "no arguing" didn't they get? "Because the Pack females are giving me shit, that's why."

Ben nodded. "We know that, which is why we think it's important for you to be the one to go get her."

"First of all, the only reason she hasn't been brought here before this is because her doctors are in Halle. Second, the moment I show up, *informally*, with the Luna, the females are going to start giving *everyone* shit."

"They're demanding full protocol?" Dave looked shocked.

"No. *Gina* is demanding full protocol."

The three men exchanged a look. The strongest Wolf female, Gina had been vehement in her outrage over a non-Pack Luna, and her loud protests were stirring up the other females. Nothing would do but for Rick to follow *full* protocol, forcing the Pack to accept his mate as their Luna. The fact that Gina was Dave's sister made things even more awkward for the men.

"Shit. Sorry, man."

Rick eyed Dave with some sympathy. "Not your fault." He was beginning to wonder if it wasn't time for Gina to go start her own Pack, somewhere far, far away. Like in Alaska. "But because of Gina, I need you two to go get Belle."

The men nodded, all argument tabled. "I'll protect the Luna, Rick. Don't worry." Ben grinned. "Although from what I remember, she may not need much in the way of protecting."

"She can't shift, remember? Not until Doctor Howard says the pin can come out, and he told me it will be another six months before that happens."

"How's her physical therapy going?" Dave's concern was written all over his face.

"It's going well, but I've been warned she's been pushing herself a little harder than she should be." And when Belle found out he'd been monitoring her progress, she was going to be seriously pissed at him.

Not that he cared. Her Alpha had forced him to leave her behind four months ago, citing her injury. He'd agreed, reluctantly, his Wolf howling in protest at the thought of leaving his mate. Now, his patience was at an end. Phone calls were not enough to still the raging in his blood for his petite, fiery, *injured* mate.

Belle was coming home, if he had to fight the Pride Alpha and his own Pack bitches the entire fucking way.

Belle stood outside her small apartment, one small suitcase in hand, ready to bid the town of Halle, Pennsylvania a somewhat fond farewell. All of her other belongings were already winging their way across state to the Poconos thanks to a trio of very enthusiastic Wolves. They'd shown up on her doorstep as promised, cheerfully packed all of her belongings into a truck and driven away, leaving her only her bed, a folding chair and a small dinner tray. They'd even taken the television. She had the feeling if she hadn't hidden her little computer they would have taken that, too.

She shivered and wished Richard would hurry the hell up. The forecast had mentioned snow, and her hip ached like a son of a bitch. All of her belongings had been shipped the day before; the only thing left was good-byes.

Not that there are many of those to be said, which is why the farewell is only somewhat fond. Her parents had long since retired to Arizona; she'd talked to them more than once over the phone, but their relationship was distant at best. They hadn't even bothered to fly down to see her in the hospital, and as far as Belle was concerned that was a good thing. The Alphas and Betas of the Pride were there to see her off, and Sarah had sworn she'd be here, as had Adrian and Sheri. They'd yet to show, but Belle had faith that they would. These people here, and the man who waited for her, were the ones that mattered.

None of the other Pride members could be bothered, and Belle decided that, too, was a good thing. She had a limited supply of pepper spray, and the gun shop owner had told her that, without a license, she couldn't get a gun.

God alone knew when *that* would come through. Until then, she'd make do with her more makeshift weapons.

"Give me that." Max, the Pride's Alpha, took her suitcase out of her hand with a frown. "Sit in the Durango and get warm."

She opened her mouth to argue and saw Emma in the car, waving her over. "Fine." She blew her blonde hair out of her eyes and limped to the SUV, trying desperately not to lose her balance on the icy pavement. *Fuck.* She could feel the cold seeping into her bones. *Why couldn't Rick live in the friggin' Bahamas?*

"Belle."

Belle smiled. "Simon." She automatically looked behind him for Becky; the two were rarely far apart unless they had to work. She found Becky settling into the Durango next to Emma, and grinned. Sarah sat there too, waving at her. She wondered when the other woman had arrived. How had she missed it?

He placed one hand under her elbow, steadying her on the ice. "C'mon, let's get you in the car before you fall on your ass."

He gently steered her towards the car, his body hovering

over hers protectively.

She hoped they got to the SUV before Richard showed up. Simply mentioning Simon's name was enough to earn her a growl. If he saw how solicitous Simon was being, he'd probably have an aneurysm.

"Thanks, Simon." She started to settle into the seat, gingerly putting weight on her hip.

"Hey."

She looked up into dark brown eyes that had once defined her world. "Yes?"

"If anyone hurts you, let us know. We'll come up and kick some dog ass for you. Okay?"

Belle blinked back tears as Max, Emma and Becky all nodded their agreement. "Thank you." She leaned over and took Becky's hand as Emma's landed on her shoulder. "Thank *all* of you."

Simon nodded. "We're Pride."

And as far as they were concerned, that said it all.

Belle couldn't hold back the tears, burying her face in her gloved hands. Only a handful of people still considered her Pride, but they were the most *important* people. She knew now she'd always have a home here, and friends, no matter what happened.

Soft arms circled her shoulders. "Remember what I said, Belle. Everything will be all right."

She sniffled as Sarah, bless her heart, stroked her hair.

"Just keep picturing how Richard's going to react to the full Brazilian you got!"

She gave a watery chuckle just as Simon said, "Really? A full Brazilian? Ow! Damn it, Becky! What did you do that for?"

Her shoulders shook as Becky started chewing on her

mate. "What the hell are you doing picturing Belinda bare?"

"I'm not! I'm picturing *you* bare!"

"Ew. I'd rather eat honey-covered ants."

Emma groaned disgustedly. "It's not that bad, you big pussies."

There was dead silence.

"What?"

"Emma!" Max looked like he was strangling on a laugh.

"What?"

Simon's big, bellowing laugh had Belle lifting her head from Sarah's shoulder. Becky was laughing so hard she was snorting. Sarah was trying desperately not to giggle and nearly biting her lip through in the process.

"What did Emma say that has you all laughing so hard?"

Simon moved, revealing Adrian and Sheri, grinning, standing by the side of the SUV.

"What makes you think it was me?"

Adrian's amused snort said it all.

Belle leaned around Sarah. "She called us all big p-pussies for not getting full Brazilians."

Sheri turned her back on the SUV. Her shoulders were suspiciously rigid.

Adrian blinked slowly. "Well. Spank my ass and call me Morris."

They were still laughing when the Wolves pulled up five minutes later. Two men got out of the huge SUV they were driving. "Ms. Campbell?"

Belle stepped out of Max's Durango with a little help from Simon, fully expecting to see a big, angry redhead sitting in the driver's seat of the other vehicle. "That would be me."

The man smiled and bowed his head. "Luna. I'm David Maldonado, Rick's Beta, and I'm here to escort you home."

Belle felt her face freeze. No one was in the driver's seat. *Oh, Rick, you'd better have a good reason for ditching me again.*

And this time she wasn't going to buy "Your Alpha made me do it".

"Explain to me, *again,* why Rick couldn't be here?" Belle stared out the window at the passing scenery, struck once again by the beauty of the rolling hills and mountains. She'd been in the Poconos once or twice before, for vacations, back in the day when she still took those. Back before things had gone horribly wrong. The Pocono Mountains were a ski and resort area in Northeastern Pennsylvania, a southern part of the Catskills mountain chain, and was roughly two hours away from Halle. Belle was pretty sure if it hadn't been for Max telling Rick to stay away, Rick would have come to visit since two or so hours would have been no hardship on the Wolf Alpha. But she knew if he'd visited, he would have carted her off to the mountains with or without Jamie Howard's approval.

Ben sighed. "Gina, the current dominant female, is demanding full protocol when you arrive. This means that Rick *has* to be there, waiting for you."

Belle took a deep breath, already knowing she was going to hate Gina. *Thank God Rick sent me that package.* She'd read enough to know how important protocol was to the Wolves. "And what am I supposed to do?"

"Wait for Rick to greet you and welcome you into the Pack. Have you read over any of the material he's sent to you?"

She had. She'd rather read stereo instructions, but she had. "Yes."

"Good." The obvious relief in Dave's voice would have been

insulting if he hadn't added, "We want to make sure that you're as safe from Gina as you can possibly be, at least until you're up to accepting challenges. Hopefully by then she'll have given up on the idea of becoming Luna."

Belinda saw the skepticism on Ben's face. "How many of the females currently follow Gina?"

The two men exchanged an uneasy look. "The most powerful ones."

She turned to stare at Ben, who was driving the land yacht they'd picked her up in. She'd never been in a Suburban before, and hoped to hell this wasn't Rick's car. There was no way she'd feel comfortable driving it. "And the others?"

Their silence was telling.

"I see." *Bullies, bullies everywhere, and I can't shift yet. Wonderful.* Not for the first time, she resented Jamie's insistence that the pins remain in her leg for another six months. If she didn't leave them in she risked having a bad limp for the rest of her life. If she waited to have the pins removed, once she shifted the bones would heal completely, and she'd be mostly pain-free.

"How soon can I expect Gina to challenge me?"

The men stared out the front windshield, their silence uneasy.

"Wonderful." *I gave up Frank's burgers for this?*

Rick dressed in his best silk shirt and his darkest jeans. As he pulled on his black boots, he noticed his hands were shaking. "Fuck." He took a deep breath, determined to meet his mate as a strong male, not a whimpering, shaking fool.

Belle was the only person on the face of the planet capable of tying him into knots. He'd come to crave the sound of her voice before he fell asleep at night. The conversations they indulged in were his lifeline in a world where his Pack was still in transition. She'd by turns confused him, amused him, given him advice and been the verbal shoulder he leaned on, whether she knew it or not.

And Gina, the bane of his existence, was determined to do everything in her power to see to it that, without *her* by his side, he could not run the Pack, despite his announcement of having found his Luna and mate in Belle.

Rumor had it she'd been down in the Lodge's archives, researching God-knows-what. He decided to have someone keep a closer eye on her. The woman was more trouble than she was worth, and if it hadn't been for Dave he would have already exiled the evil bitch.

When he'd first taken over, he'd been glad of the assistance she'd given him, grateful that someone was willing to take on the difficult task of controlling the Pack females. But Gina had taken things further than that, practically creating an Amazon Pack, and God help anyone she deemed weak or unworthy. By the time he'd figured out what was going on, he'd met Belle, and the balancing act had begun.

If he ever wanted his Pack to acknowledge his mate as Luna, he could do nothing to interfere with how she dealt with the females. All he could do was deny Gina's every request, refuse to see her, and defer all of her questions to "the future Luna".

To say Gina was pissed would be an understatement. A number of the weaker females had shown up bruised and bloodied at the Lodge's clinic in recent weeks. Ben was rapidly running out of patience; if Rick didn't get Belle installed soon, certain female heads were going to roll, and damn the consequences.

He stomped into the living room of his apartment, making sure his boots were firmly on his feet. He plucked his heavy leather jacket out of the closet and put it on, ready to face whatever his Luna had in store for him.

He only hoped Dave and Ben had been able to make her understand the situation. His playful kitty could be stubborn at times. He headed into the elevator and punched the button for the lobby. He had most of his shaking under control by the time the elevator stopped.

The doors opened. Immediately he wished they would shut.

"Hello, Rick."

His Wolf growled as the Pack's dominant female sauntered up to him, daring to stroke his arm possessively.

"When is your little mate due to arrive?"

"The Luna will be arriving shortly. Take your place with the other females."

Her eyes narrowed angrily, but the smile never left her lips. "I look forward to meeting your mate, Rick." She tried to loop her arm through his, not at all deterred when he pushed her hand off. "I'm sure she and I will get along just fine."

She blew him a kiss, laughing huskily as she glided out the front doors of the lodge.

"God, I hate that woman."

"Amen."

He turned, not surprised to see Graciela Mendoza hovering by the elevator. She was sporting yet another bruise on her cheek. He could see red finger marks, recent, around one slender wrist. Her expression was sullen and defiant. "Please tell me the Luna is going to eat that *puta* for breakfast."

Rick nearly choked. He'd never heard Chela curse before.

"Sorry."

He sighed as Chela's head dropped, her shoulders hunching inward. Her small defiance appeared to be over. "Go outside and wait for the Luna, Chela."

Her curt nod was swiftly followed by her jerky exit. Not even her breeze touched him as she gave him a wide berth.

He followed her out, determined to keep Gina away from his mate, at least until he had a chance to properly mark her as his.

After that, unfortunately, she was on her own.

Chapter Two

Belle stared as they pulled up to Rick's "home". "Wait. It's a lodge?" Rick had failed to mention that during their long conversations. Everything they spoke of had revolved around Pack, Pride, her injuries, and whatever else had popped into their heads.

You'd think the fact that the man owns a freakin' ski lodge would have come up in conversation at some point during the last two months...

Ben was grinning with pride as Dave nodded. "Yup. We're not as popular as some of the bigger lodges around here, but we're one of the best." He carefully maneuvered the tank Belle was beginning to think of as Big Bertha up the driveway. It was plowed and sanded, something Belle was grateful for. "We cater mostly to people who don't want the experience of the larger runs, and crowds, but still want a relaxing week of skiing."

"What are the facilities?"

Dave's brows rose at her professional interest. "Two ski runs, one bunny, one intermediate. We have a four-star restaurant we're hoping will someday become five. We have a spa on-site. There are rooms in the main lodge, as well as cabins that can be rented on the west side of the mountain. The east side is reserved for the Pack and their families, all of whom work for the lodge."

She stifled a laugh as the lodge's sign came into view. "Red Wolf Ski Lodge and Spa, hmm?"

Ben grinned. "Like it?" He chuckled when she snorted. "Most of the big ski resorts around here shift into water parks for the summer, but people mostly come here from New Jersey, New York and Philadelphia for the skiing. Recently we upgraded some of our facilities to be more wheelchair accessible.

"We have a full gym, a day spa, babysitting services offered by some of the Pack females, and even a small golf course. All of it sits on about three thousand acres, a third of which is forested. Hiking and horseback riding are popular in the spring in this area. We just warn the humans to beware of wild animals. Right now, our only guests are shifters; Rick arranged it that way because...well, you'll see."

She stared at the huge wood and stone building. It looked like a mountain cabin on steroids. It was long, two stories high, with a vaulted, dark grey rough barely visible under the snow. She could see the doors of the hotel rooms through the railings of the huge deck that ran all around the second story. "Where are the cabins?"

Ben took one hand off the steering wheel and started pointing. "The cabins are around the back. If you follow the road to the right, it leads to them. Follow the road to the left, and it takes you to our banquet facilities."

She turned back to Dave. "Banquet facilities?"

"Winter weddings are pretty popular up here. Wait until you see the room. With the fairy lights lit, it looks like a winter wonderland."

Ben flicked a glance at Dave. "Damn, Dave. You're such a girl."

Belle covered her mouth before Dave could see her smile.

"What?"

"Fairy lights?"

"Isn't that what they're called?"

"Yeah, but... I mean, real men don't say *fairy lights*. Call them Christmas lights, or, I dunno, string lights."

"Are you questioning my masculinity?"

"All I'm saying is, if I see you dancing around in a tutu, I'm not gonna be surprised."

"Asshole."

"Fairy."

"I'm gonna kick your ass when we get out of the Pack meeting."

"You can try, Tinkerbell. You can try."

Belle leaned forward. "Dave?"

"Hmm?" He stopped glaring at Ben long enough to turn towards her.

Belle grinned and kept her voice low, but not so low Ben couldn't hear her. "I think he likes you."

She sat back and waited for the explosion.

"On, no. No way." Ben's face was beet red as he pulled up outside the lodge.

Dave leaned over, an evil look on his face. One hand fumbled the door open behind him. "Admit it, sweetie. You want my ass." He blew Ben a kiss before hopping out of the truck, sprinting for the front of the lodge before Ben could even turn the truck off.

Ben scowled after the Beta as he exited the car. Belle smirked as he opened her door and held out his hand, his eyes still on the figure of the Pack Beta as he took his place next to Rick. The Pack Alpha stood surrounded by his people, men, women and children waiting to welcome her to her new home. A tall brunette woman stood next to Rick, too close for comfort in Belle's opinion. The smirk on the taller woman's face brought up her hackles. Her resemblance to Dave marked her as his sister, Gina.

"Oh, c'mon, Ben. You have to admit, he got back at you." Belle accepted Ben's outstretched hand as he helped her out of the SUV.

Ben's jaw ticked as she watched him reach in and grab her cane. "Yes, he did."

She put her hand on his arm, suddenly concerned. "It was a joke, Ben."

He took a deep breath and bowed slightly. "I'm aware of that, Luna." His expression was more relaxed as he handed her cane to her and threaded her free hand through his arm. "Dave doesn't always know when to stop pushing."

Belle frowned thoughtfully as Ben assisted her to the Lodge. *What the hell is going on there?* She looked back and forth between the two men. *Huh. Maybe Ben really* does *want Dave's ass.*

Her speculation was abruptly halted as Rick stepped forward. That waist-length red hair was blowing freely in the wind. His ice blue eyes were glued to her face. The scar along his left cheek was pale against his wind-kissed skin. He was so hot she felt faint.

Right. That's why I left Frank's burgers behind.

No one would ever think to call Rick a handsome man. Tall, broad, intimidating, with hawk-like features, he radiated danger on a visceral level. Belle shivered under the intensity of Rick's stare, her chin rising in unconscious defiance.

Rick smiled, feral, hot, and possessive. He stood before her, tall and proud, looking down at her with burning satisfaction. "I welcome you, Mate and Luna, to your new den. May our cubs—"

"Kits."

His smile faltered. She raised one brow, demanding he acknowledge the change.

His expression warmed. "*Children*, be strong and healthy, nurtured by our Pack *and Pride*." His smile turned to a grin as she regally nodded her acceptance of his phrasing of the old, traditional greeting.

The growl of the dark-haired female right behind Rick did nothing to deter her from making sure that the Poconos Pack understood that they were now a mixed-race Pack.

Rick continued, his gaze never leaving hers. "May your strength be our strength. May your courage be our beacon on moonless nights. May your wisdom guide our paws to the right trail." Rick took her hand as the rest of the Pack knelt on the porch. All except Gina, who smirked and crossed her arms.

When Rick turned and saw Gina standing there, he snarled.

"You can't force me to accept a crippled cat as my Luna, Rick."

Belle took a step forward, heedless of the warning hand Rick laid on her arm. "Are you challenging me?"

Gina smirked. "Yes."

Belle smiled sweetly. "According to Protocol, you must withhold challenge until the injury that prevents me from shifting is resolved."

The smirk fell off Gina's face. "What?"

"As the injury was sustained in defense of my Pridemate, it is considered a badge of honor. Therefore, you have no choice but to withhold challenge until I can shift and face you on an equal footing."

"Just because you decided to save the fur of some worthless pussy I can't challenge you. Is that what you're saying?" Gina took two angry steps forward before a voice stopped her.

"The Luna has correctly cited protocol."

Belle looked up to see a bruised, battered female step forward. Her dark brown eyes were full of loathing as she stared at Gina.

Gina growled and turned on the smaller woman. "Excuse me?" Some of the other Pack females took places by her side, five in total, all of them growling at the now cowering woman.

"*Gina.*" Belle closed her eyes as Rick's deep, commanding voice flowed over her in a sensuous caress. She opened them to find the Pack bowing before him as he stood on the bottom step. He towered over Gina, a soft mist whirling around his feet. Belle felt that soft mist touch her ankles and nearly groaned at the erotic sensation.

The Pack female was desperately clutching her head and trying to stand. Rick's expression was cold as he stared down at her. "You demanded full protocol. Now you will abide by full protocol. Are we clear?"

Gina growled, but Rick stood unmoving. The females surrounding Gina tugged on her, and Gina bowed, acquiescing to her Alpha.

Rick backed up and slipped his arm around Belle. He addressed the Pack, his power flowing over them, an intimate caress against all of her senses. "I introduce you to my mate, Belinda Campbell, your new Luna."

She wasn't certain who let loose the first howl, but it was swiftly followed by another, then another, until the entire Pack, other than Gina and her band, were welcoming her with their song.

Belle grinned, lifted her face, and showed them why Pumas were called mountain screamers.

She tried to hide it, but he could tell his little mate was stunned at the look of the lobby. "We tried to go for a Northwest feel for the lodge without losing the urban touch. Do you like it?"

He watched as she turned in place, taking in the red leather club chairs, the geometric red, brown and tan rug, and the dark leather sofa. Dark walnut end tables were scattered between the chairs with tall wrought iron lamps providing reading light. Huge wrought iron chandeliers illuminated the space. Dark walnut exposed beams were a rich contrast to the creamy yellow walls and the pale fieldstone floors. The check-in desk was the same dark wood touched with rich golden accents, as were the elevator doors across the lobby.

"It's beautiful."

Rick couldn't stop from beaming at her. "Thanks. I helped decorate it." His smile dimmed as he remembered the frequent arguments he'd had with the old Pack Alpha over renovating the dying Red Wolf Lodge. The old man had refused to see what was right in front of his face. If they lost the Lodge, the Pack would be forced to move, something Rick wouldn't tolerate. Rick had eventually been forced to challenge him, even though it grieved him to do it.

The old Alpha had put up a hell of a fight. Rick reached up and touched the scar on his cheek. To him it was a badge of honor, and a salute to the man who'd held their Pack together for nearly thirty-five years. Now the old Wolf was sunning his days away in a house in Arizona, his mate by his side. Rick couldn't wait to take Belle out to meet the old coot. His grandfather was going to *love* her.

"Where's our cabin?"

He blinked and looked down at his mate. Her shoulder length blonde hair sparkled from the beginnings of a fresh fall of snow. He missed the longer length she'd had the last time he saw her. He hoped she was willing to grow it back out. "We don't have a cabin. We live in the Lodge."

Her nose wrinkled. "That won't be very private, will it?"

"We have our own elevator up to the third floor. That entire floor belongs to us."

Belle's jaw dropped. "The entire *floor?*"

He nodded to the front desk clerk, pleased when the woman merely nodded back rather than baring throat. She was checking in a couple who'd just arrived and, even though it was a shifter couple, he wanted everyone who worked with the customers to act as human as possible. It was a habit they'd lost long ago, as his grandfather kept the Pack, and the Lodge, as isolated as possible. "We hold private, employee-only functions up there as well." He slid his keycard through the lock on the door behind the counter marked "Employees Only". Once the door shut behind them, he led her down the hallway towards the elevator in the back, ignoring the doors to either side.

"Wow, this is fairly nice for an employee area."

He grinned. "What were you expecting, a dungeon?"

"I'm not sure, but it wasn't that you'd carry the lobby into the offices." She poked her head into Ben's office, waving at the Marshall. "Hi, Ben."

He grumbled something under his breath, his cheeks turning red. Rick frowned, wondering why his Marshall wouldn't look him in the eye. "Ben—"

"Bye, Ben."

Rick allowed his mate to tug him away, seriously curious now as his mate's shoulders began to shake. "What did you do to Ben?"

She looked up at him with wide, innocent green eyes, so startling against her fair skin. "What makes you think I did anything to Ben?"

He frowned at her, not fooled for a moment. "Belle."

She laughed as he opened the elevator, pressing the button for the third floor. "Well, it all started with fairy lights."

"Fairy lights?"

"Uh-huh. Seems Dave really likes them."

Rick nodded slowly. "I don't get it."

"Do you want to?"

He thought about Ben's red face. "I'm not sure."

The elevator doors opened and they stepped out. He growled at her wince as she stepped forward. "You're in pain."

Her smile was extra toothy. "Yup. I'm going to be in pain for at least six more months, too. Get used to it, big guy."

Rick picked her up and strode down the hallway to a set of double doors. He ignored her weak attempts to get free, only easing his grip when she gasped. "Sorry."

"Put me down, Fido."

He stopped just outside the double doors and glared at her. "You bite me and you'll regret it, Belle."

"Oh, I'm so afraid," she cooed. "Watch me shiver in my boots."

And the amazing thing was, she *wasn't* afraid of him. Not one tiny little bit. If anything, she was getting seriously pissed off at him.

He loved it.

Everyone was afraid of him, from small children to grown men. But Belle was no more afraid of him than she was of a gnat. A dead one, at that.

"Don't make me break out the rolled-up newspaper."

If her hip hadn't been broken he would have dumped her on the floor for that one. "Don't worry, sweetheart. I've made sure the place is just the way you'd like it. I even got your litter box all set up for you."

He set her down as she bared her teeth and hissed. He opened the door and waved her in with a laugh. "Welcome home, Belle."

She shivered as that deep voice washed over her. *Welcome home, Belle.*

Home.

She stepped over the threshold, eager to see Rick's idea of *home.*

She stopped, shocked at what she saw. She'd expected him to continue the theme he'd had in the lobby up here, since it so clearly matched his tastes.

Instead, he'd built something straight out of Casablanca. Dark, rich woods with brown, tan and green textiles in tropical patterns littered the living room. The exposed wood of the sofa and chairs had richly carved fronts and sported "pineapple" feet. The side tables and coffee table were also exquisitely carved. The drapes were pale ivory, a contrast to the mocha latte walls and exposed, dark beams. The floor was the same wood as the furniture, with a large sisal rug underneath to define the area.

She could see the intricate dining table and chairs beyond the living area, as well as a kitchen that would make any serious chef swoon. Because the whole area was so open, instead of feeling dark and dreary the living space felt open and earthy.

He'd even painted the ceiling a soft, barely-there blue, finishing off the look nicely.

"Is there anything you'd like to change?"

She looked around, taking in the stone and wood fireplace, the massive entertainment center with the plasma screen TV, the bric-a-brac and photos that lined the wall...

Wait a moment. "Rick, when did you start hanging my pictures?"

"I did that yesterday. I wanted you to feel at home as soon as possible."

Big dope. She didn't know whether to sigh or to hit him. "You went through my things?"

He rolled his eyes and stepped past her into the living room, shutting the door behind them with a very final sounding *click.* "It's not like I read your diary or jerked off in your underwear. I hung a few pictures, that's all."

She bit back a snarl as he hung up his jacket. "They are still my things. You can't just go through someone else's things." *What if he found my medical bills?*

He stalked towards her. His hands curled around her shoulders, halting her progress when she tried to move back instinctively. "I didn't 'just go through someone else's things'. I went through my *mate's* things."

"Without her permission." Her chin went up, daring him to deny he'd done something wrong.

"*This* is all the permission I need." His mouth swooped down, taking hers in a kiss that set her soul on fire.

Soul afire or not, they needed to get a few things straight.

She picked up her foot and slammed the heel of her boot down, hard, on his instep.

"God damn mother-fucking son of a bitch!" Rick howled, hopping back from her, his face completely blank with shock. "What did you do that for?"

She leaned on her cane, trying her best to keep her expression serene in the face of his growing anger. "You do not go through my things. You do not open my mail. You do not answer my cell phone unless I ask you to. You do not read my e-mail. You do not go through my checkbook." She stopped for a moment, mentally counting up the things she didn't want her overbearing mate to stick his big nose into. "You can take my car to be inspected. All insects shall be slain by you. If I have a doctor's appointment, you may drop me off, but I won't have you there growling at the nurses or my physical therapist, so you'll go do shopping or Pack things until I'm done. You will not *forbid* me to do anything, or you'll live to regret it. 'Nair in your shampoo' type regrets." Not that she'd ever go through with that threat. His hair was truly beautiful, and she'd sooner cut off her own arm than one single inch of it. "Oh, and one other thing." She reached up and patted him on the chest. "The Halle Pride leaders are my friends, okay? So I want you to stop picturing Simon's balls in a pickle jar in your fridge." She smiled up at him, all sweetness and light, not surprised by the fact that his face had gone expressionless.

"Is that all?"

"Not quite. You're going with me to Florida in April. You'll need to buy a suit."

He pulled her jacket off, his jerky movements betraying his lingering anger. "Why is that?"

"Emma asked me to be a bridesmaid, and I said yes. One of the garment bags brought up here should be my dress, in fact."

"I already own a suit."

She sniffed, knowing how it would annoy him. "I'll have to see what it looks like." She tried to saunter into the living room but was hampered by her limp.

His long suffering sigh followed her as she made her way into the bedroom.

Holy moly. If the front of the home had been full of decadence, the bedroom eclipsed it entirely. Sapphire blue silk mixed with burgundy on a four-poster bed so massive it would swallow her five-foot-six-inch frame whole. It looked like something out of a tropical bordello.

"I can't wait to see your skin against all that silk."

Belle turned to find Rick standing behind her, so close she was surprised she didn't feel his breath on the back of her neck.

She did feel it when he leaned down and licked a slow, torturous path from her shoulder to her ear, stopping to nibble at the sensitive juncture where her neck and shoulder met. Without even thinking she tilted her head, giving him better access.

His hands went around her waist, holding her steady as he nibbled and sucked to his heart's content. "I have a few ground rules, myself."

"Hmm?" Belle opened her eyes, only then aware she'd closed them. The ruby silk had turned a deep brown, letting her know her eyes had changed. Her Puma was purring as her mate's scent surrounded her.

"Fuck, that's sexy." His low growl against her neck sent a shiver down her spine.

"What ground rules?"

Is that my voice? Even at his best, Simon had never gotten her to whimper, and Rick had barely touched her!

She could feel his smile against her neck and knew he'd heard it. "My rules are simple." His hands slowly lifted the hem of her black turtleneck. "Rule number one. When we're in the bedroom, you have to be naked."

She dropped her cane as he pulled her sweater up and over her head, tossing it carelessly onto a fringed, backless chaise done in the same sapphire blue as the bedding. At least she thought it was blue. It was the same shade of brown as the blue parts of the bedding.

His hands began a slow caress of her breasts through the lace of her bra, paying special attention to her nipples. "Rule number two: when it comes to your health, I *will* be involved. Get over it. And I already paid your medical bills, so get over that, too."

She would have protested, but he chose that moment to unclasp her bra and pluck at her bared nipples.

His hair cascaded over her shoulder, brushing her breasts and belly with butterfly touches. "Rule number three." His hands began smoothing down her stomach, heading for her black slacks. "I will stop picturing Simon's pickled balls when I know for certain you're completely mine."

Belle turned in his arms, not surprised by the fierce, possessive scowl on Rick's face. She reached up and stroked his cheek. "I'm all yours, Rick."

His hands stilled at her waist. With a muffled oath he picked her up, buried his face against her neck, and bit.

Belle screamed as the pleasure-pain ripped through her. Her claws dug into his shoulders, earning a growl from her Wolf as the orgasm rolled through her with the force of a freight train. She jerked in his arms, her good leg lifting to wrap around his waist, her pussy grinding against his rock-hard erection through her slacks and his jeans.

When his teeth pulled out of her shoulder she groaned in regret, only to scream again as he bit down in a different spot with a rough snarl. He howled against her flesh as she bit back, right through his silk shirt, claiming the man who held her so tightly she knew he'd never let her go.

Chapter Three

Rick couldn't stand it any longer. He pulled and tugged her slacks as gently as his growing sense of urgency would allow, unwilling to cause her a moment's pain. He longed to just use his strength to rip the damn things from her hot little body, but he retained enough sanity to know how much that would hurt her hip.

So he unzipped, and unbuttoned, and *thank God*, pulled them down those long, luscious legs of hers. The boots she wore flew as he toppled her onto the bed face first, that incredible ass of hers right in his face. He moaned out loud at the sight of the black lace thong she wore.

She tried to stand up but he stopped her, placing one hand between her shoulder blades, the other at her waist. "Stay down." He knew his smile was wicked as she snarled, those bright gold eyes of hers glaring at him from under the fall of her pale hair. "Don't make me spank that pretty little ass of yours, Belle."

The red sheets had turned gold, almost the same shade as her Puma's eyes. It was one of the reasons he'd picked that color, knowing what he'd see when his vision changed. He'd had more than one erotic dream centered on what he was looking at right now, in fact.

He stroked her under her thong, reveling in the gathering

damp between the bare folds of her pussy. She was getting off on this, big time.

He used his strength to keep her down, pulling one hand away long enough to unzip his jeans and free his cock. "Are you ready for me, Belle?"

She opened her mouth—

The phone rang. His private number, the one used only by the Pack. He closed his eyes, willing whoever it was to *go away*. He had a mate to fuck, and he wasn't about to stop unless the Lodge was burning around their ears.

Hell, the Lodge could burn merrily as long as he was between her thighs when it happened.

He slid the head of his cock past the thin line of her thong, pushing gently into her swollen pussy. "Take me, Belle."

She snapped at him, those sharp, pointy teeth of hers still in evidence. Claws ripped into the bedspread under her hands.

He stopped, totally shocked. *My little kitty has been holding out on me.* Wolves had the power to shift between wolf and man; no Wolf could stop in between, never mind what the myths about his kind said.

Now he knew where some of those myths had come from. In self-defense he leaned over her, grabbing both of her hands and forcing them flat against the mattress.

He growled as she bucked under him, furious and delighted as she fought him for dominance. *Him!* He was twice her size, and she *still* tried to throw him off.

She was the most incredible woman he'd ever met, bar none.

He moaned as her jostling forced him deeper inside her. "Oh yeah, baby." He snarled, his own fangs dropping as he fought the Wolf for dominance and won, barely. "Submit."

She stilled. "What?"

He grabbed her wrists and forced her arms apart, causing her upper body to lay flat against the mattress. He slid even further inside her, his Wolf demanding he dominate his mate. His cock was now halfway inside her. Her moist heat was nearly his undoing. "Submit to me."

"Oh, Fido. Them's fightin' words."

He would have been worried if he hadn't heard the humor threading through the threat. He leaned down, letting his hair form a curtain around them. Distantly he heard the answering machine pick up, but really couldn't give a...well, okay, he *was* giving a fuck, wasn't he? He brought his lips to her ear. "Submit to me."

He felt the shudder that ran through her, saw the hot, speculative gleam in her eyes, before his pretty little kitty turned into a wildcat in his arms.

She bucked against him, writhing, her claws moving in and out as she tried to toss him off and out of her body. He held her as still as he could, trying to put as little weight as possible on her hip, only forcing the issue when she grunted in pain.

"Enough!" He held her down, immobile, his body trapping hers against the mattress. His cock was now fully seated in her body, throbbing with the need to move before he exploded like a teenager with his first hot pussy. "Submit, Belle."

"Never!" She bucked one last time, but he could see the exhaustion beginning to war with the need.

Time to end this. "Submit, my Luna." He moved back cautiously, the smooth, silken glide of her snug passage nearly his undoing.

"I submit—" his heart jumped into his throat, "—that you're crazy."

He slammed his cock home, smirking as she gasped and shuddered. "Submit, Belle." He pulled back again in a long, slow glide.

"Ah, I submit my taxes every year."

He could feel her shoulders shaking as she grinned up at him.

He grinned back, slamming his cock home again. "Submit." He didn't even have the heart to growl it. He was no longer sure which of them was submitting to the other.

"I submit to a gynecological exam every year, too."

He nipped her shoulder as he rammed into her, reveling in her sighed moan. "Submit, love."

She looked up at him through her bangs, shocked. "What?"

He backtracked. He hadn't meant to reveal that yet. "Submit, Luna."

She smiled slowly, bucking back into him as he fucked into her again. "Make me. *Alpha.*"

With that one insolently drawled word, Rick lost control of his beast, and thanked God for it, too.

Oh my God! Belle felt Rick lose it as he began ramming his cock in and out of her wet pussy. She yowled and pushed back, trying her best to get him even deeper, not caring in the least that she sounded like a cat in heat. He bit savagely into her shoulder, once again claiming her and marking her for all to see as his. She shrieked, her orgasm nearly robbing her of breath, the Puma in her glorying in the strength of her mate.

He let go of her hands to grab at her waist, heedless of her hip, pulling her back into his thrusts like a wild man. "*Submit.*" His voice was deep and gravelly, like he battled his Wolf back.

She couldn't fight him anymore. She collapsed beneath

him, allowing him total access to her body.

"Mine."

She withheld that one, final thing that would tip him over the edge, knowing it would mean all the more when she finally gave it.

He reached under her body, between her legs, and began stroking her clit, timing it to coincide with the motion of his hips. When she moaned hungrily he picked up speed. "*Mine!*"

She could feel herself building up to one hell of an orgasm. She bit her lip, determined to save that one final word for when she came.

"Say it"!

"Yours!" She could barely get the word out as her body clenched around him in a climax so strong it robbed her of breath.

When he howled out his own release she couldn't even move, so satiated with pleasure she couldn't have said her name if her life depended on it.

All she knew was she was his.

Rick collapsed over her, too stunned to do more than pant.

Where the hell has she been all my life?

He could feel himself beginning to snarl as he remembered where, and with whom, she'd been. He took a deep, calming breath, amazed at the depth of rage in him at the thought of her with any man but him.

His Wolf mourned the fact that he hadn't been her first. The man rejoiced in the fact that he would be her last.

"Ow."

He headed into the bathroom without even stopping to

think. He had an Ibuprofen and a glass of water in hand before he even realized he'd moved. He shook his head at himself in the mirror and chuckled.

So this is what it's like to be pussy-whipped.

He decided not to share that little observation with Belle. She'd probably do something gruesome to him in his sleep.

He wet down a washcloth and added it to his pile to bring his hurting mate. He carried everything back into the bedroom, smiling to see her exactly as he'd left her. He put everything down on the end table but the wet washcloth. "Hold on one moment, and I'll have you comfortable."

"Mm-hmm."

He would swear she purred as he gently cleaned her off. He was just glad she couldn't see the bruises he'd left on her hips, or the multiple bite marks he'd left behind. They would heal, given a few days, but everyone would know she'd been most thoroughly claimed.

He got rid of the washcloth after cleaning himself up. Picking up the bed's control, he pressed the button that lifted her side of the mattress.

"What the hell?" She opened her eyes and stared at the remote in his hand. "You got me the extra deluxe hospital bed?"

He shook his head. "It's one of those beds you see on TV. I can raise your legs or back, depending on what's most comfortable for you. Didn't you see that the sheets are two twins?"

She blushed bright red and glared up at him sleepily.

"I mean, your face was right there." The devil was in him tonight, it seemed. He wanted to see her all feisty again. "It's not like you could miss it."

He laughed when she snarled at him, swiping at him halfheartedly with her claws. "You just wait until I can feel my legs again, you bastard."

He smirked. "That good, was I?"

She rolled her eyes as she accepted the pain pill he held out. She sipped the water, swallowing the Ibuprofen. "Uh-huh." She sighed dramatically as she snuggled down into the bedding, her breasts jiggling under his delighted gaze. "But you know I'm the best you've ever had, so I think that makes us even."

He had no intention of telling her she was right. She was smug enough as it was.

Belle listened in as Rick made a few phone calls. He thought she was asleep. She had been, up until the Ibuprofen wore off.

"Yeah, Gina tried calling last night. Like I was going to answer the phone on my mating night." He paused, obviously listening to the person on the other end. "No, I want you to show her every aspect of the restaurant." He sighed. "Chela, just do this for me. No, I don't give a flying fuck what Gina thinks." He chuckled. "Good girl."

Maybe I should bring a Milk-Bone for Rick's friend. Belle tamped down the unreasonable jealousy she felt over his call to another woman.

"Just remember, Belle is in charge. Any changes she wants to make are pre-approved by me."

What? Belle sat up slowly as what Rick was saying filtered through the haze of pain that had woken her in the first place.

She could see him slowly pacing, a slight frown on his face as he listened to whatever Chela had to say. "Uh-huh. No, I took care of the paperwork two weeks ago."

What paperwork? She felt her heart trip as possibilities,

good and bad, ran through her mind.

"This is her dream, Chela. Help me make this happen."

Whose dream? She was practically screaming in her mind, wondering what the hell her mate was up to. She totally hated not knowing what was going on.

Rick froze, his gaze darting to the open bedroom door. "I'll see you in a bit." He hung up the phone and walked into the bedroom, his eyes turning brown as he saw her sitting up. "You should be asleep, my Luna."

She bit back a smile. "You think I can sleep through big clumpy feet stomping around the dining room?"

He slid beneath the sheets, one hand coming to rest on her bare stomach. "I was quiet."

She tapped one of her ears. "Cat hearing." She sniffed. "*Much* superior to *dog* hearing."

She giggled when he growled and nipped at her breast playfully. "*Dog* hearing?" He started to tickle her but stopped as soon as she grunted. "You're in pain, aren't you?"

She nodded, biting her lip to keep from screaming. Her hip hurt like a son of a bitch, no offense to the man next to her.

Rick practically ran for the bathroom. She could hear him slamming open cabinet doors and running water. He came back and helped her take the pain pills, frowning until she'd finished the glass of water.

Mumbling to himself, he left the room, returning with two graham crackers. "Eat."

She looked up at him suspiciously. "The doctor told you about my stomach, didn't he?"

Two imperiously raised eyebrows demanded she eat.

"Fine." She nibbled the crackers as his expression relaxed. He was right, anyway. The amount of Ibuprofen she'd been taking had done some damage to her stomach, but they'd caught it before it became a full-blown ulcer. "Thank you." She batted her lashes up at him. "You're my heeero."

He threw his head back and laughed. "I'm sure I am." He sat on the edge of the bed, gently brushing her hair back from her cheek. "I want to be."

She gulped. The yearning in that normally hard face had her reaching up. His beard, soft as silk, grazed her palm as she stroked his cheek. His eyes closed in pure bliss, his head leaning down until she was scratching at the top of his head. "Typical canine."

"Hmm?" He was barely lucid, turning into her hand. If he'd been a cat he would have been purring.

"You have a happy spot."

He grinned, his eyes never opening as she continued to scratch. "Give me a few minutes and I'll pet *your* 'happy spot' until you purr."

He leaned down to kiss her. Just as their lips met, the doorbell rang.

Belle looked over at the clock. It was seven in the morning. "Expecting someone?"

"Yes." He grinned wickedly. "Get dressed. I have a surprise for you."

Belle stood, wincing as she put weight on her abused hip.

"Here."

She took the underwear he handed her, pausing to watch him pull on his jeans. She nearly groaned as she realized he'd be walking around commando all day.

She looked down at the panties in her hand, then looked back at him. With a smirk she tossed them onto the bed, then pulled on her own jeans.

His groan was music to her ears.

She pulled on the lacy bra and reached into her bag for her favorite shirt. It was a men's style button up in a pale blue pinstripe with wide collars and cuffs. She covered it with a low scoop sweater in sapphire blue.

By the time she was pushing her feet into her low heeled boots Rick had the door open.

"Chela. What's wrong?" The worry in his voice was barely audible, but it let her know something wasn't quite right.

"Sorry, Rick. Rumor has it Gina's planning on starting trouble at the restaurant today. If you want me to introduce the Luna as the new manager, we'd better make it quick."

Belle stumbled, pulling up short against the doorjamb.

Manager?

Rick looked over his shoulder and started towards her. "Where's your cane?"

"Um..." Belle looked behind her into the bedroom, still dazed.

He shook his head, gently lifting her aside. He went in, got her cane, and handed it to her on his way out. "I want you to meet Graciela Mendoza, Chela to the Pack." He followed Belle's slow progress into the living room, his gaze riveted to her white-knuckled grip on the cane's handle. "Chela, Belle."

The woman bowed and bared her throat to Belle, something that would take some getting used to. "Luna."

Belle nodded back, uncomfortable in a way she hadn't been yesterday. Rick was watching her, his gaze sharp. "Chela." She put out her hand, expecting Chela to take it.

Chela looked at it, slowly standing to look her in the face. The bruises marring her skin were numerous.

The dark-haired woman blinked before reaching out slowly

to take Belle's hand. "It's a pleasure to meet you, Luna."

The uncertainty in her voice tugged at Belle. "It's a pleasure to meet you too."

Chela nodded, the gesture abrupt and tinged with fear. "If you'll follow me, I'll take you down to the restaurant."

"Wait, Chela." Rick strode into a different room, off to the right of the bedroom. He emerged pushing an electronic scooter, complete with basket, in candy apple red. "Here."

Belle looked at the scooter, then looked up at Rick. "I can walk."

"I know. But you're in a lot of pain today, and you'll have a *lot* of walking to do. When your hip gets tired, use the scooter to get around."

Belle was stunned. She knew how much the damn things cost. She'd looked into it once, but her COBRA insurance had denied her claim and she hadn't been able to afford it on her own. They didn't seem to understand that you couldn't push yourself in a wheelchair with a broken arm. She'd had to rely on Sarah, Sheri and Adrian to get around. Now that her arm was healed, she could use a standard wheelchair, but he'd spent a couple grand to make her life easier, knowing she'd only need it for a few more months. What kind of man did that?

He smiled like a kid when she settled into the seat. "The controls are simple." He leaned over her and pointed at the handle bars. "Forward, reverse, and horn. The headlamp comes on automatically when you move." He turned it on and watched as she learned to maneuver around the apartment. She could feel his gaze burning into her, the pride on his face visible to any who looked.

She stopped next to him and climbed off the scooter. "Thank you." She wrapped her arms around him, cuddling in close, trying without words to let him know just how much both of his gifts meant to her. Not only had he done everything in his power to see to her comfort, he'd handed her dream to her on a silver platter. She had no clue how he'd found out she'd always wanted to run a restaurant, but she wasn't about to turn the gift down. No one had ever done anything like that for her before. It made her feel...cherished. She was going to have to make sure she did something for him, something that would show how much he meant to her. She'd just have to figure out what that something was.

He hugged her back, his face buried in the crook of her neck. She felt him smile just before he placed a small kiss there. "You're welcome." He let go and winked at her. "Have a good day at work, my Luna."

She watched as he strode out of the apartment, that incredible hair of his swishing above that equally amazing ass.

When the door shut behind him she turned to Chela. "Where can a girl get breakfast around here?"

"So, that's the general layout, all of the financial paperwork, and the employee records. What do you think?"

What do I think? I think I want to kill Gina Maldonado, that's what I think. Gina had been acting manager of Lowell's Steakhouse for the past year, and she'd pretty much run it into the ground. Key staff had quit, preferring to work the front desk rather than be under Gina's thumb. The financial records looked like they'd been done by a toddler.

But what really, *really* pissed her off was the fact that she'd signed certain documents as Gina Lowell.

Belle had learned a few things in the last four months. First, she'd learned who her true friends were. Second, she'd learned that, distance notwithstanding, Rick Lowell was *hers*, damn it.

And third, she'd learned that she had zero tolerance for self-absorbed assholes with delusions of grandeur. *Been there, done that, thank you very much.*

Belle looked up and met Chela's gaze. "Does Rick know any of this?"

Chela shook her head. "He's been avoiding Gina ever since he realized what she was up to."

"Up to?"

"Trying to forcibly become Luna."

Belle tapped her nails on the wooden desk. "And how was she doing that?"

Chela hunched in on herself, becoming nervous. "By beating up the lesser females and surrounding herself with the strongest. Making sure she was the one who made the decisions normally made by the Luna, citing the fact that she's the dominant female and Rick *had* no Luna." Chela's shoulders relaxed as she refocused on Belle. "At least, not until now."

"And don't you forget it." Chela's startled laugh was sweet. "So we need to deal with Gina, first and foremost." Belle tried to discreetly squirm in her chair, but the pain in her hip was steadily growing. *Looks like the Ibuprofen wore off again.*

Chela frowned as Ben entered the office, a glass of milk in one hand and a small plate in the other. "Luna. Chela." He put the plate and glass on Belle's desk with a smile. On the plate were two pain pills and some graham crackers. "Rick asks you to meet him for lunch, if your schedule permits."

Belle smiled at Ben. "Thanks. I'll meet him." *I don't think I'll ever get used to how formal the Woof-Woof set is.*

"He also wanted to let you know there's going to be a Pack meeting tonight. If you're not back at the apartment by six, he asks that Chela escort you, as the meeting is at six thirty."

Belle saw Chela nod to Ben before he smiled at both women and left. "If Ben knows you're in pain, you can bet Rick does. You might want to take that."

She'd forgotten that, as Marshall, Ben could feel the physical well being of each and every Pack member. He'd know quickly if her medication was wearing off, and knowing Rick, he was under orders to let him know if Belle was trying to hide her pain. Belle quickly took the medication. The last thing she needed was Rick breathing down her neck right now. "Okay." She leaned forward, her expression intent. "You're Pack. Born or made?"

"Born."

"So you have a pretty good idea about what will get Gina to back off, right?"

Chela nodded. "Total annihilation."

Belle was silent for a moment. "So talking things out diplomatically won't work, huh?"

Chela ran her hands through her hair, a hopeless look on her face. "Gina Maldonado wants to be you. She wants to be Luna, and she wants Rick. Always has, always will. If she can find a way to get rid of you without harming Rick, she'll do it. If she has to share you with Rick, she'll do it. And if she can kill you without it killing Rick, she will."

"Oh."

"I know things are different in the Prides."

You think? In the Pride a female like Gina would have been Outcast long before now for her treatment of the "weaker" females. Not that any of the "weaker" females would have stood for it. They would have found many, many ways to make Gina's life miserable...

"I know that grin. The Grinch gets that grin every

Christmas on my TV."

Belle motioned Chela closer. "I have *a plan.*"

"Does it have tweezers, very hot water, and Sea Breeze astringent in it?"

Belle waited, hoping Chela would explain what the hell she was talking about.

"Um. Never mind."

"Oh, no. You can't just let that one sit in my brain and percolate."

Chela choked on a laugh. "My father made my mother very, very angry one day before he went to work on a big project."

"Uh-huh. Men do that to women."

"He called her from work and told her he was very sore after a long day, and that he wouldn't be back until the next day."

"Why not?"

"He works construction in New York, and the drive can be murder when you're hurting. Anyway, he asked what he could do to soothe his muscles."

"Oh, boy."

"Yeah. She told him to take a very long, very hot shower, as hot as he could stand. Then, when he got out, he was to splash Sea Breeze all over his body."

"But...that would..." Belle's eyes widened as she realized exactly how much pain splashing astringent into wide open pores would be caused.

"Yeah. He had to sit in a cold tub for *hours.* He called her and cursed her in three different languages and didn't come home for a month."

"Didn't that cause problems?" Now that she'd lived with

Rick, even if it was only for a day, she couldn't imagine spending a month away from him.

"Oh, yes, but his other mate went up and took care of him. Then she and Mom got into a fight—"

"*Other* mate?"

Chela gulped, and Belle wondered exactly what her expression looked like to make the previously friendly woman look wary. "Yes. It happens sometimes, that a Wolf finds he has two mates."

Not my mate.

"It's very rare, though, and unfortunately was the cause of a lot of my parents' fighting."

"Where are they now?"

"My mom lives in Santa Fe. My father and Brenda live in Texas."

"So they don't live together?"

Chela shrugged. "My father flies up to see my mom once a month. Now that they don't have to live together, they actually get along fairly well. My mom doesn't have to take care of him anymore; Brenda does all of that."

"Huh."

Belle started when she felt Chela's hand on her arm. "Don't worry about it, Luna. Rick has only one mate."

Belle felt her anger drain away at Chela's touch, felt the brush of the other woman's power as it soothed her Puma. She looked at the other woman in wonder as the knowledge of what was going on moved through her with swift assurance. "You're the Omega."

Chela's hand drew back, her expression startled. "What?"

What? How the hell... What the...

It was like knowing Rick's eyes were blue, or that drinking water would quench your thirst, or that Gina Maldonado was a bitch in both senses of the word.

Belle bit her lip, wondering how to fix what she'd just blurted out. She knew she was right, but how to make Chela see it? "Trust me, nobody these days takes me from pissed to pleased with just one touch."

"Not even Rick?"

She shook her head slowly, watching the other woman's face carefully. Belle wasn't certain how to make Chela see what was so clear to her. "Do me a favor, will you?"

"Sure."

Chela still looked wary. She'd have to fix that. "I want you to think, *really* think, about how the Pack feels right now."

Chela's head tilted to the side and she frowned. "How the Pack feels?"

"Are they angry? Are they upset? Who's fighting right now? Who's in need of a shoulder to cry on?"

Chela's brow furrowed.

"C'mon, Chela, I know you know the answer. I can feel it in you." Belle felt something strange moving within her as she concentrated on Chela. "Tell me."

And that something whipped out of Belle and wrapped around Chela, cocooning her in Belle's strength.

Chela's eyes blanked. "Gina is supremely pissed, and heading to the restaurant. Her flunkies are spoiling for a fight. Rick is distracted. Not sure why. Ben is..." Chela looked startled before a muffled laugh erupted. "Um. Not going there."

Huh. Go Ben. "How does the Pack as a whole feel?"

Chela's eyes slowly focused back on her, a wide smile lifting the corners of her mouth. "Hopeful."

Belle matched Chela's smile. "We need to talk to Rick. And I have an idea of how to deal with Gina."

"You do?"

"Uh-huh." Belle outlined her plan to the new Pack Omega. The look of wonder on Chela's face was a balm, but the unholy glee that eventually replaced it was even better.

Just as she stood to get settled into her scooter, Chela's hand landed on her arm. "Luna?"

"Yes?"

"Thank you."

"You're welcome."

Rick stepped into Lowell's, prepared to meet Belle for lunch, and stopped cold.

Gina was hovering over his mate, snarling at her, right in the middle of Lowell's dining area. Patrons, shifters all, watched with amusement as Belle stood there, her expression one of vapid confusion. The scooter was right behind her, what looked like paperwork shoved willy-nilly into the basket. Her cane rested against the seat as she stood under her own power and faced her rival.

"Who authorized these changes?"

Belle looked innocently baffled. "I did."

Rick grinned at the sound of his mate's voice. He stepped back and prepared to be entertained, crossing his arms over his chest and leaning back against the wall.

Gina had no idea what was about to happen, and he had no intention of enlightening her. He'd been on the receiving end of *this* mood often enough that there was no way he could not recognize it.

"You had no right." Gina was speaking through clenched

teeth, never a good sign in a Wolf. It made him wonder how long his mate had been playing with the alpha bitch.

"Oh, but I did. Rick made me not only manager, but part-owner of Lowell's." She smiled sweetly.

Ah, my curious little cat. I thought she'd find those papers.

Gina drew in a deep breath, her fury obvious. "He had no right to give you what is mine!"

"I believe it is the Alpha's right to gift his Luna with whatever he wishes."

Rick's eyes widened as Chela boldly stood beside his mate, her gaze never leaving Gina's face.

One of Gina's minions moved forward, but Gina held up a hand. "Well, someone's getting brave." The sneer on her face as she stared at Chela was met by a cold glare.

"I wouldn't if I were you." Belle's gleeful sing-song words went right past Gina.

"Perhaps you need a lesson in who's boss around here." Gina stepped forward, her arm lifting, her hand clenched into a fist.

Belle's hand shot out so fast Rick barely saw it move, grabbing Gina's wrist and stopping Gina's fist an inch from Chela's face.

The most interesting thing was, Chela didn't even flinch. She just kept that cold, steady gaze on Gina. That fixed, dead gaze was starting to give him the willies.

Gina howled in pain as Belle smiled vacuously. "I *really* wouldn't try to hit Graciela any more, okay? That's bad." She shook her finger at Gina, who was desperately trying to get her wrist out of Belle's curled hand. "Bad woof-woof."

Half the patrons of the restaurant had their faces buried in their napkins, their shoulders shaking. The rest were openly laughing.

Rick scented blood and realized his kitty had unsheathed her claws right into Gina's arm. Her pretty green eyes had turned bright gold. Her expression was still as vapid as she could make it. A cheery smile graced those full lips as she put her free hand in her pocket.

Gina managed to get her arm free of Belle's grasp. "Bitch."

"Oh, silly poodle. I'm not the bitch, you are, remember?" Belle shook her head sadly. "Didn't your mommy teach you *anything?*"

Rick swiped at his mouth, desperate to wipe the grin from his face as Gina shook with anger. To be defeated by someone she considered inferior was bad enough, but to be defeated by someone who was acting like a complete imbecile was intolerable to someone like her.

"Why you little—" Gina lunged forward, losing what little self-control she had.

Only to be brought up short by the air horn Belle pulled out of her pocket and set off right next to her ear. The dominant female dropped, hands over her ears.

Belle let up on the button. "Not done yet." Belle's cheery voice floated through the sudden silence, causing more than one patron to choke out a laugh.

Mental note: take Belle's new toy away. Rick's ears were ringing from halfway across the room. He could only imagine what Gina and her coterie felt like. With another quickly hidden grin he realized Chela had covered her ears, muffling some of the sound.

"So, here are the new rules, okay?" Belle looked dementedly happy as she started ticking things off on her fingers. "No more trying to piddle on Rick's carpet. If anyone's going to mark territory there, it's me."

74

Gina snarled up at Belle but rapidly pulled back when Belle brandished the air horn.

"No more beating up on the other women or I will take you to the vet and have you tutored."

"Neutered." Gina corrected her with a frown.

Belle leaned down and patted Gina's cheek. "Don't worry, sweetie, *someone* would learn *something*."

Rick coughed as Belle straightened. He lost his fight with his grin as she winked saucily at him.

"And last, but not least, you will show deference to the Omega. Because if you don't, you *will* regret it in a very bad, not good, terribly awful way." She was really laying on the inane sincerity. Rick wondered what she was up to, and how much in damages he'd probably have to pay.

Gina bared her teeth at Belle. "Who's the Omega?"

"Me." Chela's grin was not in any way friendly.

"You?" Gina's laugh reminded Rick of a hyena, especially when her loyal minions joined her.

There was a gasp as Belle rapped Gina on the nose with...

Rick lost it. His Luna had just hit the dominant female with some rolled-up papers she must have grabbed from her scooter.

God I love that woman.

"Bad woof-woof." Belle shook her finger, completely ignoring Gina's shocked expression. The alpha covered her nose with her hands. "No Milk-Bone for you." Belle gave Gina that horrendously serene, vacuous smile, and Rick tensed. "Now, remember. The Omega, that's Graciela for those of you with two-second scrolling memories, outranks all of you. So," she clapped her hands together, setting off the air horn for a brief, shrieking moment of pain, "I want you to treat her with respect."

"No."

Belle looked sad as she shook her head. "Oh, honey, you're just not the quickest bunny in the forest, are you?" Someone snickered. "It's not me you need to be afraid of."

Gina stood, her sneer not nearly as pronounced as it had been. "No?"

"Nope. Well, okay, *sometimes* you need to be afraid of me. But not right now."

"Then who do I have to be afraid of? Rick?"

"Nope." That scary cheer was there again.

"Then who?"

Belle sighed, and looked at Chela. Chela never took her eyes off Gina.

Gina's face went white as Chela let Gina and her friends have it with both barrels. Rick had no idea what Chela was doing to them, but it did *not* look pleasant. Gina was soon a sobbing wreck on the floor, curled into a ball of misery, and her friends weren't any better.

"Now remember, poodles, the Omega outranks everyone but the Alpha, Luna, Beta and Marshall." Belle tapped Gina on the head with the rolled-up papers. "That means you. So I would treat her with respect, or this could become a daily, perhaps an *hourly*, occurrence around here."

The savagely gleeful anticipation on Chela's face let him know that she would probably use any infraction of the Luna's new rules, intended or not, to inflict pain on Gina and her minions.

"Now shoo. I have a lunch date." Belle waited patiently while Gina and company beat a hasty retreat.

Rick caught one glimpse of the dominant female's face as she left, and his blood ran cold. He pulled out his cell and called Ben.

"Ben here."

"Keep an eye out for the females. Belle just put a verbal smack-down on Gina and the woman looks like she might be out for blood."

"Will do. Enjoy your lunch."

Rick hung up and made his way over to his Luna, shaking his head at her antics.

"I *really* don't like her."

He took her hand and led her to a seat. "Don't worry. No one would ever be able to tell."

Chapter Four

Belle stood there, shivering her ass off in the cold night air, and wondered what the hell was going on.

Rick, his arms crossed, stared at the gathered Pack intently. The Pack grunted, Rick nodded. Then there was silence as his gaze drifted over them.

Belle looked back and forth at the group of silent people, all of them eerily staring back at Rick. She could see the occasional person nodding, or in Gina's case, sneering. Then Gina flinched and glared at Chela, who smiled smugly back.

What the fuck is going on?

She started tapping her foot, fidgeting the change in her pants pocket. She stared up, watching the stars twinkle through the break in the trees. She huffed out a bored breath.

"Belle?"

She turned to Rick, startled to see the Pack was gone.

"Aren't you coming?"

"Coming where?"

He looked shocked. "We're heading back to the Lodge for drinks, to celebrate our mating."

"Um. We are?"

"Yes."

"When was this decided?" Belle could feel her temper beginning to spike, and it felt good. She'd never dared lose her temper in Halle for fear of losing her so-called friends.

And just look where that got me.

No, it definitely felt good to let go. Witness how Gina had gone out of her way to avoid her all day! There were definite perks to this lack of anger management.

"Just now." He looked genuinely confused, and a little concerned.

"You didn't say anything."

"I spoke to the Pack."

Her eyebrows rose into her hair. "When?"

He stared at her intently for a moment, a look of shock passing over his face. "You didn't hear me, did you?"

"*When?*" She was moving beyond annoyed to seriously ticked.

Rick blew out a breath, running a hand through his hair. "C'mon. I'll explain it on the way in." He put a hand under her elbow and started walking. "I have a mental connection to every Pack member."

"Yeah, so does every Alpha."

"No. I mean, I can hear them, and they can hear me."

"Of course they can." She patted his arm soothingly.

"No, Belle. I mean, like telepathy."

She stopped. "In their heads?"

"Yes."

"Can you read my mind?"

"When I try to, or when you think something very loudly, yes."

She growled.

He held out his hand commandingly. "Give me the air horn."

Damn. She handed over the air horn with a frustrated sigh. "You never let me have any fun."

His expression softened as she pouted up at him. "If I had known, I would have mentioned it earlier. We've only been mated for a day."

They started walking again. "So from now on the Pack meetings will be held verbally. Problem solved."

"Problem *not* solved."

"Why not?"

"Because I can't hold the Pack meetings verbally."

"Why not? Some ritualistic bonding thingie that you're not going to explain because I'm a cat and I'd never understand?"

"Ritualistic bonding thingie?"

The indulgent amusement in his voice grated on her rapidly fraying temper. *"Rick."*

He snorted, a smile flirting around the corners of his mouth.

"Why can't you hold Pack meetings verbally?"

"Tradition holds that all Pack functions held by the Alpha be done mentally."

She let her mouth move into her sweetest smile, mentally crowing at the worried look that crossed his face. "But I can't hear you when you do that."

"I know." He patted her hand. "I'll make sure to fill you in after the meetings."

She could feel her teeth trying to grind together and did her best to relax. From his wince, she didn't think she'd succeeded. "How am I supposed to function as Luna if I can't hear you?"

"I'm sure we'll figure something out."

They were almost at the Lodge. Belle smiled again, delighted when she felt him shiver under her hand. "Yes. I'm certain we will."

Belle felt insanely giddy as Rick carried her into their apartment after their mating party. The best part? Gina and company had chosen to skip the event.

She was still humming "Little Red Riding Hood" as Rick took her straight into the bedroom. Dave was completely insane once you got a few mojitos into him. He'd actually gotten up on a table and begun to sing that. He'd been leering at Ben the whole time. He hadn't stopped even when Ben turned his back on him and walked away.

"You, my Luna, are plastered."

She giggled and aimed a kiss at Rick's mouth. She hit his chin. "Oh, scratchy." She reached up and stroked a hand over his cheek, feeling his beard. It felt good against her palm. She spared a thought to how it would feel on the flesh between her thighs.

Rick groaned. She wondered if he'd heard her thoughts. From the flush creeping up his face, she thought he might have.

She thought about it harder and felt herself getting wet.

"Bedtime, little kitty."

Belle pouted as he put her on top of the comforter. "What if I'm not sleepy?" She shimmied a little bit, trying to entice him into the bed.

His eyes turned brown. "Belle..."

She sat up and slowly pulled off her sweater and dropped it to the floor. His gaze was glued to her fingers as she began slowly unbuttoning her blouse. She made sure to have her fingertips linger at her breasts as she pulled the shirt away from her chest. The shoulders slipped down and hung on her elbows. She looked up at him from under her lashes and licked her lips.

He growled, his fists clenching. "You need to rest."

"I can rest. After." She allowed the top to fall off her, her hands moving to the front clasp of her bra. "Did you know the chemicals released during orgasm can help control pain?"

His gaze left her breasts to collide with hers. A wicked smile was beginning to curl his lips. "So orgasms are good for you?"

She nodded, giving him her most innocent, come-hither look. She bit her lip and unclasped the bra, allowing her breasts to spill free. Her nipples were already beaded in the cool air. "And you don't want me to feel any pain. Right, Rick?"

"What? Oh. No. No pain."

His absent tone nearly made her laugh. She held the seductive pose with some difficulty. Her fingers slipped to the snap of her jeans. He whimpered as she drew the zipper down as slowly as she could.

She bit her lip to keep from grinning as he rushed to remove her boots. He stood and dropped them to the floor, staring as she shimmied out of her tight jeans.

He gulped as her bare pussy was revealed. She didn't know if he'd forgotten she'd gone without panties that morning.

He nearly tripped over his own feet as he hastily ripped his own clothing off. She finally allowed the grin to break free as she leaned back against the pillow and began absently stroking her clit.

"Dear God, woman. Are you trying to kill me?"

She moaned in response, shutting her eyes as the sensation of her own fingers stroking her pussy began to overwhelm her. She wanted desperately to thrust her hips upwards to increase the sensation but knew better than to try it.

She felt the bed dip as Rick joined her. His big hand covered hers, stopping the motion of her fingers. Now it was her turn to whimper.

"Allow me." One long, strong, thick finger entered her, finding just the right spot to rub against. She gasped as she flung her head back against the pillow. He took advantage of her exposed neck, sucking and biting hard enough to leave a mark. The scrape of his beard only heightened her pleasure, sending shivers down her spine as his hand stroked her closer and closer to orgasm.

His mouth left her neck and worked its way down to her breast. He suckled her, harder and harder, matching the rhythm of his finger to the rhythm of his lips until she had no choice but to move against him.

"Uh-uh. Stay still." His hand left her pussy to press at her hip, stilling her movements. "No pain, Belle."

"You're kidding me, right?"

His wicked grin flashed across his face; that glorious red hair of his was golden brown, letting her know her eyes had definitely changed. "I'm going to fuck you until you don't remember your own name, but *only* if you stay perfectly still."

"I'm not sure I can stay still." She reached up and brushed her hands across his furry chest. "Besides, you know how much you love it when I buck back." She tempted him again with a glimpse of her tongue against her lips, loving how his grin faltered.

It didn't take long for the grin to return. "You're right, I do." He picked her up, ignoring her squawk of surprise, and placed her feet on the floor. He turned her around, pushing her shoulders until her face was once again buried in the bedspread.

"Y'know, Fido, there's more than one position. Even for a dog."

"Belle."

She could hear the laughter in his voice as he took hold of her hands, holding her down. The head of his cock nudged the opening of her pussy. "There's the cowgirl position." He sputtered a laugh as he began to slowly push inside her. "Then there's the lap dance position." He began slowly fucking her, nibbling on her neck, and she started to lose her train of thought. "There's, um, missionary. Yeah, miss...oh, right there."

He nipped at her neck sharply, causing her to see stars. She needed him to bite her in the worst way. "Any others?"

"Others? Oh, right. There's...can't you go any faster?"

He slapped her ass and she yelped. "How fast would you like me to go?"

She began slamming back against him, setting the pace. "How's this?" She panted.

"Good." His voice sounded strangled. "Very good." He began matching her stroke for stroke, building the fire between them. "You're gonna make me come, my Luna."

"Oh, God, Oh God." She chanted with each thrust. "It's so good."

"Come for me, Luna." He let go of one of her hands and reached between her thighs, flicking her clit as he bit down into her shoulder. He pierced her skin with his teeth, growling. She screamed, coming so hard his cock nearly got pushed out of her pussy.

Her Wolf howled as his hips jerked, coming so deep inside her she swore she could taste him.

She barely felt him pulling out, picking her up, and placing her on the comforter. She was asleep within seconds, thoroughly sated, a contented smile on her lips.

Rick was surprised at how quiet things had been, considering how furious Belle had been the night before about the whole telepathic thing. Although the make-up sex had been amazing, he was surprised she'd decided let it go. She'd gone to the restaurant that morning with a cheery wave and a smile after they'd finished breakfast. She even let him know she was planning on working through dinner. She'd made a face when he told her about the Pack meeting that night, but she'd agreed and, feeling that she'd somehow let him off easy, he let her go without any further interference. He got the feeling that perhaps the Pumas didn't get together as often as the Wolves and made a mental note to discuss that with her.

And here she was at the Pack meeting, all bundled up warm and cozy. He'd brought her a lawn chair to sit in, hoping to ease the pain he knew she was in. He planned on taking her home after the meeting, tucking her in under a nice, warm blanket, and personally massaging every inch of her sweet, creamy skin.

He began slowly opening his mind, allowing the others into his thoughts. He could hear each of them quieting their minds, preparing themselves for his nightly speech.

"WHO LET THE DOGS OUT! WOOF! WOOF! WOOF! WOOF!"

Rick flinched, his eyes nearly crossing, as the loud, grating music poured into his mind from...

Oh, Belle. You are in deep, deep shit.

He turned to find his mate curled up in the chair he'd brought her, her head bopping merrily to the tune coming from the iPod she'd turned on. She smiled at him cheerfully, waggling her fingers at him as her toe tapped the beat. He could hear her singing along in his head, especially the part where they sang, *"a doggie is nuttin' if he don't have a bone"*.

Rick did his best to tune out the annoying songs playing so loudly in his head, but he wasn't certain he succeeded. "How Much Is That Doggie in the Window" was bad enough, but when the K9 Advantix flea and tick jingle started going on a loop he nearly lost his temper. After a while people began rubbing their foreheads and peering at him strangely. He wondered if he was beginning to shout.

He cut the meeting short, sending the Pack off to romp in the snow, and stalked over to Belle. She was still sitting there bopping to the music. This time it was an oldie by the Monkees called "Gonna Buy Me a Dog".

Staring down at his wayward mate, he began to agree with the sentiment. A dog would be a *lot* easier to deal with than his woman.

He reached down and pulled the headphones out of her ears. Thankfully, the sound in his head muted along with the sound in hers. "Okay, Belle. Point made. Let's figure out a compromise."

"What are you talking about?"

He picked her up out of the chair and cradled her close. He'd come back for it later. "The Bimbo Barbie act might have worked on Simon, but don't ever assume I don't know *exactly* how smart you are." He watched as she blushed, her eyes turning gold in pleasure. He wondered how many times men had focused on her beauty, not realizing the sharp mind behind those gorgeous green eyes and full, killer lips.

He stared towards the Lodge, determined to work a few things out with Belle before she drove him mad. "I promise I will try to figure out some way to satisfy both you and tradition if *you* promise to never play flea collar jingles ever again."

She reached up and kissed his cheek. "Okay, Rick."

He climbed the steps into the Lodge, careful of his precious burden. "You're still not getting the air horn back."

She smirked, but the genuine laughter behind it was obvious. Belle was having fun. "You don't honestly think that was my only one, do you?"

All he could do was shake his head as he carried her back towards their private elevator. "You are a damn dangerous woman."

"You say the sweetest things."

Despite everything, he couldn't help but laugh out loud as she batted her eyelashes at him outrageously.

Rick had been upset when they'd gotten back to their apartment and found Ben standing outside their door, pain killers in hand. The Marshall had been rubbing his hip and wincing. Rick had immediately drawn a bath, undressed her carefully, set her in, and told her to stay put. She could hear him talking to Ben out front, but couldn't quite make out the words. She decided to let it go, figuring if it was something important Rick would tell her about it before bed.

The hot water had done the job almost too well. By the time he returned to help her out of the huge Jacuzzi tub, she was mostly asleep. He'd dried her off, put her to bed, and settled in next to her. He'd put his big hand on her stomach, kissed her good-night, and pretended to go to sleep. He didn't even try to seduce her.

She could tell something was bothering her Wolf. The tension took quite a while to leave his fingers. She couldn't help but wonder what was wrong, but unlike him, she couldn't hear his thoughts. When she tried to ask him, he'd laid his finger gently across her lips, shushing her quietly, before settling back down.

She placed her hand over his, stroking those long, strong fingers, and drifted off to sleep, determined to find out what was wrong as soon as possible.

Rick was gone when she got up the next morning. Whatever had bothered him the night before, he was apparently determined to keep it from her.

It seemed they were going to have to have another little chat about sharing.

She headed for the offices, ready to discuss things rationally. She was only carrying the air horn and pepper spray in case she ran into Gina again.

Really.

She smelled them before she heard them. Chela, Ben, Dave and Rick, all in Ben's office. She made her way as silently as she could, wondering if she would find them all goofing off over video games or something. She'd seen the console Ben kept in his office the day she'd first come. *Hey, if shooting space aliens relieves some of that stress Rick was carrying around last night, I'm all for him playing hooky. But we're still gonna talk.*

"We have to do something about this before Belle finds out."

The controlled anger in Ben's voice halted Belle in her tracks. *Before Belle finds out what?* She tried to think as quietly as she could, knowing Rick might hear her.

"God, I *hate* her." The venom in Chela's voice sent a shaft of pain through Belle's heart, but her next words erased it. "How could Gina do this?"

"It's the only way she could think of to get what she wants." Belle had never heard this level of ice in Rick's voice. Whatever it was Gina had done, it was bad.

"I tried talking her out of it, but she's adamant." She could hear the anger and sorrow in Dave's voice.

"Not your fault, man. You can't choose your family." Ben's voice was soothing.

"The hell I can't. She's no sister of mine."

"The sad thing? She's right. Protocol is on her side. As dominant female, she has every right to demand that Rick take a second mate to fill the slot of Luna since there's a good chance his mate is permanently disabled."

Belle listened to Chela's voice with a sense of shock. *Second mate?*

Rick growled menacingly. "I would sooner fuck Dave."

A low growl came from within the room. "Hey, no fighting over me, now. I know I'm such a prime piece of real estate, but, really."

Dave's weak attempt at humor didn't seem to go over too well as Ben spoke up. "Knock it off, asshole. This is serious. If Gina gets enough of the Pack on her side, Rick and Belle are screwed." Belle's eyes narrowed as she took a cautious step closer. "We could wind up with Gina being our Luna."

Rick sighed wearily. She could picture him running his fingers through his hair. "This must be what she was researching in the archives. Damn it." She heard a thump and wondered what Rick had hit. "How long?"

"Thirty days. If Belle can't shift and accept the challenge Gina threw down by then, you'll have to accept Gina as the Luna. It'll be your duty as Alpha."

"Don't tell me about duty. I know where my allegiance lies."

Belle felt numb. She stepped back, moving away from Ben's office as quietly as only a Puma could, wounded or not. She took the elevator back to the third floor and let herself into the condo. She went to the phone, picked up the receiver, and dialed a very familiar number.

"Hello?"

"I need your help."

Simon didn't even hesitate. "We're on our way."

She hung up the phone and headed into the bedroom. She packed a small bag, waiting for the hurt she knew was going to come. She just hoped that what she had in mind would put Gina's ambitions to rest once and for all.

And then she and Rick would have a little "chat" about duty along with the one about sharing.

Rick stared at the open closet door, the knife of pain twisting even further in his chest. Belle was gone. He could feel himself beginning to lose it as his Wolf howled in misery.

"She can't have gone far, not with that limp."

Rick turned blind eyes to Ben. "She must have heard us."

"Why didn't you warn us?" Ben was scowling at Chela as he wandered the bedroom. He stopped suddenly, stared intently at something on the bureau.

"She did, she just warned us too late." Rick didn't want anyone blaming Chela for this. It was his damn fault. He should have told Belle about Gina's bullshit move to claim him last night, but she'd been in so much pain he hadn't wanted to bother her with it.

"I think Belle didn't let herself feel anything until after she left." Chela bit her lip, looking more like the woman Gina beat up on than the Omega she'd so recently become. "I'm sorry,

Rick."

"Not your fault. Mine."

"No. Not your fault. No one's fault. Take a look." Ben pointed with his chin to the bureau.

Rick hurried over, eager to see what Ben did.

There, nestled in one of Belle's silk scarves, lay her air horn. On top of that was a can of pepper spray, a small gold necklace, her diamond earrings, and a tiny soapstone sculpture of a wolf.

Relief settled in, so swift he felt dizzy. "She's coming back."

"How do you know?"

"She left her jewelry. She's also letting me know she's safe." Rick saw the confusion on their faces. "The air horn and pepper spray are still here."

"Why does that strike me more as a threat than an attempt at reassurance?" Rick ignored Ben's murmur, knowing deep inside he was right and Ben was wrong.

He fingered the aqua silk scarf, sniffing as Belle's sent wafted from the fabric to tease his senses. "But, why did she leave? That's the question."

"Well, I can feel her now, and she's upset. I think she's arguing with someone."

Rick turned to Chela. Her face was filled with strain as she struggled to connect to the Luna. "Do you know where she is?"

"No...other than she does feel safe wherever it is."

The two men turned to each other. "Halle."

Rick pulled out his cell phone and dialed. "Where is she?"

"Hello to you too, Rick!" The cheerful voice floated through the phone.

"Emma, please. Where is my mate?"

"Which one?"

Ah, fuck. "My only."

"She's seeing Jamie Howard right now. Can I take a message?"

She's seeing the Pride doctor? Fear pulsed through him. "What's wrong with her?"

"Other than a mate who might be forced to shack up with a real bitch?"

"EMMA!"

"Okay, Jeez. No need to yell. And don't growl at me, either."

Rick sucked in a deep breath and tried desperately to calm his Wolf down.

"Oh wait, gotta run. Jamie's coming for us. Bye!"

It took every ounce of Rick's willpower not to throw the phone across the room. "She's seeing her doctor."

"Call him. As her mate, you have every right to know what's going on with Belle." Ben took the phone from Rick's hand and dialed Jamie's number.

"Give me that." Rick took the phone back and listened to the options. When the receptionist came on line, he was practically frothing at the mouth. "Where is Dr. Howard?"

"I'm sorry, sir, Dr. Howard is preparing for an emergency surgery right now. Can I have him call you back?"

Rick hung up the phone without answering. "Emergency surgery?" Rick had a sinking feeling he knew what the "emergency" was. He pocketed the phone. "Get the car ready. We're going to Halle."

"You can't, Rick. Gina will—"

Ben never finished the sentence. Rick's hand shot out, wrapped around Ben's throat, and pulled the smaller man closer. He bared his fangs as, out of the corner of his eye, his comforter turned from blue and red to blue and gold. "Get. The. Car. *Now*."

"Yes, Alpha." Chela patted his arm. He released Ben, who backed away, wide-eyed. "We'll get right on that."

Rick watched his Marshall and Omega run out of the room. He dialed Dave. "I need you to take over for a little bit. It seems something unexpected has come up in Halle, and I need to take care of it."

"Yes, Alpha. Don't worry, I'll make sure nothing happens until your return."

"Thank you, Dave."

He quickly gathered some things up and headed down to the lobby. He stepped into the car, ready to fetch his female and drag her back home by the top of her head if he needed to.

Chapter Five

Belle opened her eyes to the sound of a mountain lion's scream. She sighed and closed her eyes again, hoping no one would notice.

"Guys, stop fighting! Belle is awake!"

Belle winced. *Dear God, who let Emma into the room?*

She opened her eyes again to see the petite, dark-haired Curana leaning over her. The smile she wore was strained. "Can I let the big bad Wolf in now, before he eats Max?"

Belle groaned. "Sure." She shifted slightly and immediately wished she hadn't. The throbbing agony rushing up her leg was all too familiar.

There was the sound of a gasp, quickly followed by a thud. It sounded like someone had fallen to the floor.

"Hey, Belle." She tried to smile as Adrian's face swam into view, but just couldn't manage it. "Looks like you're definitely one of the Pack."

She frowned.

"I'm still standing. Ben isn't. Last I saw Rick was helping him to a seat. What did you do, anyway? Try to move?"

She nodded feebly. She'd forgotten the Marshall would feel her pain. Poor Ben. She wouldn't wish this on anyone, not even Gina.

Okay. *Maybe* Gina.

"Don't. Rick is already fighting his Wolf tooth and nail. As soon as Ben hit the ground he nearly lost. Can you imagine a red Wolf running through Halle General?"

"Which one of you screamed at him?"

Adrian made a face. "Max. He's feeling a little protective right now, and Emma decided to get in Rick's face over the second mate thing."

Belle winced. When Emma decided to let go, most people knew to duck. Rick, however, wouldn't. He'd go toe-to-toe with the Little General, which would only succeed in pissing Max off. "Send him in."

Adrian left. Belle closed her eyes and concentrated on not passing out. Nausea rose up in a wave as her hip throbbed in time to her heartbeat.

"Just answer one question. Why?"

Belle looked up into Rick's furious face. His voice was quietly lethal, and his eyes were brown. "Why what?"

His expression tightened, his fangs dropping as he growled. "Why didn't you talk to me first?"

She licked her lips. Her mouth was dry as cotton, and tasted horrible. "Why didn't *you*?"

He took a deep breath, throwing his head back. She knew he was struggling to keep his Wolf contained. *"Belle."*

"I am your *Luna*, Rick." She was losing her battle with the pain. Soon she'd have no choice but to summon a nurse. "You can't keep things from me that affect the Pack, not if you want me to actually *be* the Luna."

He studied her, his expression closed off, and her heart sank. He didn't understand what she was trying to do, and she was in too much pain to make him see it. "Do you want me to stay?"

His cold, formal wording hurt. "You have to do what your duty compels you to do."

Anger flashed across his face before he visibly forced it back. "I'll return for you tomorrow, after I get over the urge to strangle you."

She opened her mouth to respond, only to have her words cut off by his mouth descending on hers in a desperate kiss that told her exactly how scared he'd been. She reached up, careful not to jar her hip, and threaded her fingers through his hair. Whisper soft, it fell around her, cocooning her in his scent until she felt safer than she'd ever been.

His mouth lifted abruptly from hers and he strode from the room, tension thickening the set of his shoulders.

No! She resisted the urge to cry out to him, knowing he needed a little time to sort things out in his own mind. But, damn it, she *needed* him!

He paused in the doorway, his shoulders slumping as he turned back to her. The agony on his face reflected the agony in her body. He walked slowly towards her bed, his gaze never leaving her face, and pulled up a chair next to the bed, as close as he could get and still sit in it. Once in the chair, he picked up her hand and held it until the painkiller the nurse injected into her IV tipped her over into sleep. His gentle kiss on her palm was the last thing she knew.

"I still say you've pulled some stupid stunts, but this one takes the fucking cake."

"Look, we both know why I did this. Do you *want* Gina's socks sharing space with ours? And didn't we already have this argument?"

Rick set her down on the huge sofa, carefully unwinding the blanket from around her shoulders. No matter how careful he was, she still hissed in pain. He was afraid if he heard that sound one more time he would break.

The drive from Halle had been painful for all of them. Ben had ridden shotgun, Chela taking the seat furthest in the back. Belle had had the entire middle seat to herself.

By the time they got back, Ben and Chela were both pale and sweating. Belle never spoke, only whimpering occasionally when Rick was forced to go over a rough patch in the long drive up the mountain.

Chela had immediately gone up to her cabin, claiming a splitting headache. Ben had headed straight for the bathroom in the lobby. Rick had the sick feeling Ben had gone there to throw up. He'd felt relieved when he saw Dave following Ben, a concerned look on his Beta's face.

Belle smiled at him, a pale imitation of the expression he'd grown to love. "Can I have something to drink, please?"

Rick examined her face. Lines of strain were visible around her mouth and eyes, dark circles standing in stark contrast to the paleness of her skin. "Do you need a painkiller, my Luna?"

When she bit her lip and nodded he headed straight for the kitchen. He poured her a glass of water and grabbed the prescription he'd had filled against her protests.

He closed his eyes, the memory of her lying in that hospital bed overwhelming him. He didn't think he'd ever be able to tell her how he sat there, long after she'd gone to sleep, terrified of moving in case it hurt her. The big bad Alpha of the Poconos Wolf Pack had held his mate's hand and cried as quietly as he could, not wanting to disturb her in even the slightest way.

For a moment he thought he might wind up joining Ben in worshipping the porcelain god.

He'd known even before she'd left for Halle what his decision would be, but watching her moan in pain, through sleep and morphine, had merely cemented his determination.

Gina could go fuck herself. He was done. This was the last time the Pack was going to come between him and his mate.

He carried the medicine back to the living room, stifling a grin. She'd put on some reality TV program and was growling at the contestants.

"What are you doing?"

She made a face. "Would you look at that?"

He turned and saw what looked like a runway. A woman, model thin, was walking down it wearing the frumpiest outfit he'd ever seen in his life. *What the hell?* "I'd rather not."

"The challenge was to design something for a hot twenty-something out on the town. Instead this idiot designed something my Great Aunt Bertha would be proud to wear."

"Great Aunt Bertha?"

"Yeah, she was a real looker back in the thirties."

"Ouch."

"Speaking of ouch..." She held out her hand.

"Open up." Rick brushed the pill against her lips, not surprised that her eyes remained green. He didn't think he'd get to watch her eyes change for quite a while longer.

She opened and he fed her the pill, holding the glass steady so she could sip through the straw. "Thank you."

He decided he couldn't put it off any longer. "I've called a Pack meeting to deal with the Gina situation."

"It's a little soon, isn't it?"

He frowned at her confused expression. "I hardly think so." Getting Gina off his back would be one of the few pluses to what he had in mind.

"Okay. Just do me a favor and make sure you've got a first aid kit handy."

He blinked. He hadn't thought she'd want to be present for this. "Sure."

"What time tonight?"

"Ten. I want to make sure the Lodge is mostly shut down for the night. The few guests we have will understand an emergency Pack meeting."

She shrugged. "All right, if you say so." She turned back to her show, but not before her hand buried itself in the strands of his hair brushing against her thigh.

He settled in on the floor and watched her stupid show with her, totally at peace for the first time in three days as her fingers played with his hair.

Belle hated the outdoor Pack meetings, never more so than now. Pumas did it right; they held them indoors, with wine, cheese, and more importantly, *heat.* She could barely stand, even with the help of Rick's arm, her cane, and the six Ibuprofen she'd gulped on the way out the door. But he was right. Gina needed to be dealt with as soon as possible, before she'd gathered too much power. She'd already acquired more than her fair share. "Good evening, my Pack." The Pack jumped as Rick spoke out loud. Only Dave seemed unsurprised. "I called this meeting to deal with the challenge Gina Maldonado laid down before my mate, Belinda Campbell."

The Pack looked back and forth at one another, obviously confused. She knew they were aware of Gina's challenge, so she could only assume it was the fact that Rick had chosen to address them out loud.

"Due to the fact that my mate is currently unable to shift, Gina has also issued, as dominant female, a proclamation. If Belle cannot change forms within one months' time, Gina must be declared Luna of the Pack."

Ominous silence greeted that pronouncement. Only Gina and her flunkies looked pleased. Gina smirked at Belle.

Belle smiled back sweetly. Gina's smirk faltered.

"If Gina was to be declared Luna of this Pack, I would be forced to accept her as my second mate."

Belle's smile deepened, showing her suddenly sharpened teeth. She felt her claws rip through the fabric of her gloves. *Damn. Those were leather, too.*

"In light of the fact that I have more desire to bed a grizzly bear than Gina Maldonado—" Rick ignored the snickers, and Gina's fierce frown, "—I have chosen the only course open to me."

Belle shot Rick a sharp look as his shoulders straightened. Suddenly she knew what he was about to do.

She couldn't allow that. Rick was the best thing that had ever happened to the Red Wolf Poconos Pack. She took a step forward, already prepared for what was coming.

"I am ready to face Gina Maldonado's challenge."

"BELLE!"

She ignored Rick's roar as she stepped forward, letting her cane drop to the ground. She heard several of the Wolves surround Rick, and only hoped they were restraining him. She sneered at Gina, feeling nothing but contempt for the she-Wolf. "I'm ready to bring it, bitch. What about you?"

Gina laughed and stepped forward, her posse right behind her.

"Uh-uh-uh." Belle shook her finger at the females. "This is

between Gina and me. No back-up singers allowed."

"Which means your 'friend' can't help you either."

Belle took a deep breath and removed her coat. "I've gotten used to that."

"Damn."

Belle shook her head and looked back at Chela. "Down, girl. It's my turn now."

"Look out!"

Belle turned and caught Gina's fist just before it landed on her face. She sank her claws into the other woman's hand reveling in the bitch's screech of pain. She felt one of Gina's finger bones snap under the pressure from her claws. "Oh, now, *this* looks familiar."

She smiled wickedly down at the fallen Gina as Sarah's words in the diner suddenly replayed themselves in her mind. *"Everything is going to be fine. I promise you that."*

Rick relaxed as Belle's words flowed over him. *"Everything is going to be fine."*

He watched as his mate finished undressing. Gina took longer due to the wound already inflicted by Belle.

"I'm okay." He shrugged off Dave and Ben, pushing Chela's hand off his arm. He was so intent on watching the women strip he barely felt the three of them move behind him, flanking him, protecting him.

When Belle was gloriously naked she waited, hands on hips, tapping a foot in the snow. He nearly whined at the sight of the new, jagged scar on her hip but stopped himself. He would be strong for her, for what she'd sacrificed to stop Gina's plans.

Gina slithered out of her panties, stretching, trying to

tempt him with a knowing look.

He retched, then spit on the ground. "Sorry. I threw up a little in my mouth."

Gina gasped, infuriated.

"God, I love you."

Rick blinked, stunned. It was the first time Belle had thought that. Her thoughts were filled with such amused affection he couldn't doubt her sincerity. He wished with all his heart that she could hear his answer. *"I love you too, my Luna."*

Her breath hitched. The smile she turned on him was smug, cat-like, but she couldn't hide the happiness shining from her. *"I know. You show me every day."*

He blew her a kiss, crossing his arms over his chest as he settled in to watch his pretty little kitty kick the ass of one truly obnoxious bitch. He'd figure out how she'd heard him later.

She turned to Gina with a feral grin. "Let's get this over with. I'm tired of looking at your cellulite thighs."

Rick threw his head back and laughed, the sound booming through the trees, as Gina snarled at his mate.

"We can tell your ass has never seen a treadmill before, either. I mean, yeesh."

Rick laughed harder as Belle shuddered delicately.

When Gina howled, the fight began.

The women were evenly matched as they swiftly shifted. No winner there; if one had managed to complete the shift before the other, serious damage could have been done. And he had no doubt Gina intended to inflict serious damage, if not death. Belle had pushed Gina to her limits one too many times.

The differences in the sleek, powerful Puma and the aggressive, determined red Wolf were obvious to all those who watched. While Belle had the advantage of power and size, her limp remained, hampering her movements. Gina was swift and unhampered, but smaller. The two women circled each other, growling, watching with golden eyes for the slightest hint that the other was preparing to pounce.

Rick couldn't tell for certain which of them moved first. They came together in a furious clash of paws and claws, teeth ripping into shoulders as the Wolf tried to dominate the bigger Puma.

Belle's rear paw slipped, causing the Pack to gasp. She corrected, almost letting Gina push her over and onto her back. If Belle let Gina have access to her belly, the whole fight would be over.

Not that it mattered. He'd decided to walk away before the challenge. If Belle lost, he still had that option.

He stared around at his Pack. The raw anger on most of their faces was surprising. The majority of them were growling at Gina's friends. The five women nervously backed away, separating themselves from the rest of the Pack.

"She's going to win." Rick looked at the serene smile on the face of his Omega. Her eyes had a blank look to them. "Even if she loses, she's won. The Pack will no longer accept Gina as their dominant female." She looked up at him, an odd expression on her face. "I can't feel them anymore."

"Who?"

Before she could answer Gina yelped. He turned back to the fight.

Belle had gotten a hold of Gina's back leg. She shook her head, her powerful jaws snapping the red Wolf's thigh like a twig. Gina whimpered, dragging herself away from the Puma slowly stalking towards her.

Gina turned, obviously hoping to take the fight into the woods, when Belle pounced. She landed on Gina's back, forcing the Wolf's smaller body to the ground, her teeth clamping on the back of Gina's neck.

With one movement of her head she could take the life of the dominant female. She was well within her rights to do so. Half the Wolves present obviously expected her to do it. The silence in the clearing was deafening.

Gina's legs scrabbled in the snow under Belle. She fought to get the big cat off her, but it was too late. Belle was not letting go of her nemesis until she'd secured Gina's full surrender. He could see the determination in her golden eyes as she held Gina still underneath her powerful jaws.

She snarled as Gina made one final attempt to buck her off. A bead of blood dripped down into Gina's fur, making it obvious even to her that there was no getting out of Belle's hold. Gina panted her surrender, her legs going slack under Belle's weight.

Belle held on, more blood falling to coat Gina's fur, making a point none of them could miss.

When it came to a lone Puma versus a lone Wolf, the Puma would win.

Eventually Belle got tired or bored, and let go. The bitch's fur was matted with snow and blood. Belle stood over her and began slowly raking her paw through the snow over and over again.

Rick chuckled. His kitty was burying the offal.

Finally Belle was done showing her contempt for Gina. She turned her back on the Wolf and sauntered over to Rick, only the slightest limp hampering her movements. She butted her head against his thigh, purring as he scratched her behind her ears. She turned and sat by his side, cleaning her whiskers with her paw, totally unconcerned as Gina shifted back to human.

The alpha bitch was clutching her leg. "Someone help me." Her five women scrambled quickly into the center of the Pack and assisted their fallen leader to her feet. She stared at Belle, different emotions warring across her face until it settled into Gina's usual arrogance. "This isn't over."

"I'm afraid it is." Chela stepped forward. "I can no longer feel you."

Gina's face whitened.

Ben stepped forward. "She's right. I can't feel *any* of you." He pointed towards Gina's broken thigh. "I should feel that, but I don't."

Belle shifted, swifter than the first time. She stood tall and proud next to him. He quickly removed his jacket and covered her nakedness. "You are no longer members of this Pack."

Her voice flowed over him, smooth as honey, touching him in places he had never been touched before. It felt like she'd slid inside him, caressing him with smooth fingers, arousing him in ways he hadn't known were possible.

The rest of the Pack bowed before the power in their Luna's voice.

"The Pack has spoken. Challenge has been met; Protocol is satisfied. You and the members of your Pack are to leave our territory before the dawn of the day, never to return."

Rick shivered, and not from the cold. His cock hardened in his jeans, straining towards the one woman who could ease him. He slipped his arm around Belle and nuzzled the side of her neck, pleased when she tilted her head to allow him greater access.

But his mate's hard gaze never left the alpha bitch. The six women, stunned, turned away. Gina's stare flitted from one Pack member to another, looking for something, anything, that would refute what the Luna had said.

Rick allowed his power to slide along Belle's skin, delighting in her surprised gasp. She moaned and shuddered, resting her weight against him. Their power meshed, just as he'd always known it would when he finally had his Luna.

He held her easily. The two watched as, one by one, their Pack turned their backs on Gina and her Pack. A small cry escaped the woman's lips as Dave turned, a look of disgust on his face.

Gina stood, proud to the bitter end, and stared at the Alpha pair. She nodded regally before one final smirk crossed her face. "My Pack and I will be gone by morning."

Belle answered with a regal nod of her own.

Gina walked off, accepting the help of the five women who'd stood by her in her attempt to take over the Poconos Pack. No one was sorry to see them go.

Chapter Six

"Remember what I said about the surgery being the stupidest stunt you've ever pulled?"

"Yes." Belle drew her finger down Rick's chest, knowing what was coming and trying to avert it.

"I changed my mind. *That* was the stupidest stunt you've ever pulled."

"Did you really think I was going to allow you to abdicate?"

"Did you really think I was going to take Gina as a mate?"

She sighed. "No."

"Good."

Rick cuddled her closer, sighing when she squirmed her naked bottom against his rapidly growing erection.

They'd gone straight back to their apartment once they were certain Gina was gone. He'd left her clothes out in the Pack's meeting place, not even stopping for her boots. He'd just picked her up and carted her off. She was pretty sure he'd said *something* to the Pack in their heads, because they'd scattered to the four winds. She just didn't have it in her at the moment to be pissed about it.

The first thing he'd done had been to take his jacket back. He'd bundled her up in the big comforter from their bed (she was really beginning to like the big, loud thing), settled her in front of the fireplace, and proceeded to get naked. He'd pulled her into his lap and held her close for a few moments before apparently deciding she was safe. That was enough to set him off.

"But there was no way I was going to allow you to give up the Pack."

"Belle."

"Rick."

He sighed roughly. "How did you know you'd win?"

"I had a little chat with Jamie before the surgery. He assured me the change itself would be painful, but doable. And, may I say, his new nickname should be Captain Understatement? I thought he meant toothache pain, not tits in a meat grinder pain."

"You realize you're not helping, right?"

She looked up at him through her lashes. She kept her fingers moving through his chest hairs, trying to soothe her grumpy Wolf. "It dulled down to an ache once I was done, so he was right about that. After that, it was pretty easy."

"Easy."

"Yup."

He sucked in a deep breath as her fingers wandered over to his nipple and plucked.

"You know what?"

"What, my Luna?"

She looked up from under her lashes again. "There are a whole lot of positions we haven't tried yet." She bit her lip, knowing he loved it when she played innocent seductress.

His smile was slow and decadent as his eyes shifted over to brown. "So there are, my Luna." He picked her up and carried her to the bed. "Lots and lots of positions." He placed her carefully on top of the covers and opened his bedside drawer. He dropped a book onto the bed and flopped down next to her. She caught a glimpse of the cover and started giggling. "A whole book's worth."

She pointed to one of the pictures, still giggling. It showed one man having sex with multiple women. "No way. Don't even daydream about it."

He caressed one of her breasts, a happy sigh leaving his lips just before he kissed her. "Don't worry, my Luna. You're more than enough for me." He nipped at her neck. "One pussy is all I can handle."

He was up and running before the comment fully registered. "Get back here, Dick!" She climbed out of the bed, reveling in the lack of pain as she chased him into the living room.

He laughed, ducking behind the sofa. "Rick!"

"Not after that comment!"

She chased his laugher all over their apartment. He swore later the only reason she caught him was he was dying to get caught.

Only in My Dreams

Dedication

To Mom and Dad, who probably shouldn't ask me about the menthol thing.

To Dusty, who agrees to try some crazy things with me even when he's skeptical. I'm sorry for that whole menthol thing, but I still think I suffered way more than you.

To the fans of the Pumas, I hope you've enjoyed the ride. And don't worry, I'm not done with my shifters yet...

And to those who want to know, no, I will never tell the menthol story. Just mentioning it makes Dusty curl up in a ball and whimper.

Chapter One

November

"Who the fuck are you?" Gabriel Anderson, sheriff of Halle Pennsylvania, and Marshal's Second of the Halle Puma Pride, was one tired, cranky kitty. He stared at the stranger sitting in his living room and tried to remind himself that jail was a bad place for a cop to wind up in. The intruder had his feet up on Gabe's coffee table, his cowboy boots twitching in time to the video game he was playing on Gabe's Wii. Gabe kept his service revolver steady, the safety off, aimed at the intruder. To top it all off the man smelled like a shifter. "Because I like to know who the hell I'm arresting for breaking and entering."

"Wondered when you'd get in." The man's face lit up, his hands waving the remote frantically. "Hah! Gotcha, you son of a bitch." The man paused the game and set the remote on the coffee table. "Name's James Barnwell. And you're Sheriff Gabriel Anderson, Second to the Marshall of the Halle Puma Pride."

Gabe's revolver dipped slightly. "Yeah. So you know who's sticking your ass in jail."

The man stood up, and *up.* His dark blonde head easily towered a good six inches over Gabe, and at six foot two Gabe didn't consider himself to be a short man. "You really don't want to do that."

"Why not?"

The man smiled, the expression warm. His gray eyes twinkled merrily. "Because I don't think the Senate would take kindly to having one of its own in jail."

Gabe lowered the revolver but didn't relax completely. "Senate?" Why would the Senate send someone to Halle?

The Shifters' Senate was a loose conglomerate of all of the shifter species. It was traditionally headed by a Leo. The main purpose of the Senate was to see to it that humans did not learn of the existence of shifters, with the only exception being human mates. Over the years the Senate had also instituted certain laws that all shifters abided by, one of them being the sanctioning of new Packs and Prides. Every six years the different races would elect one of their own to a seat on the Senate. The current Puma Senator was an older man by the name of Harry Kirland who lived somewhere in the Midwest. Gabe had never met or spoken to the man. Max's rule was too damn new, and the Senate had a habit of giving a new Alpha a settling-in period before more than congratulatory contact was made.

It was rare for a Senate representative to visit Halle. In all the years the Halle Pride had been here there'd only been two. One was for the Puma Senator's representative to sanction the newly minted Pride. The other had been a Hunter stalking the rogue the previous Halle Marshal had eventually destroyed. Both times the man in question had been a Puma.

This man didn't smell of Puma. He smelled of Bear. "Shouldn't you be talking to my Alpha?"

"If I was here to speak to Mr. Cannon I'd be at his house, not yours." The man's smile turned to a grin. "Besides, he doesn't have a Wii."

Gabe closed his eyes and prayed for patience. "Tell me you didn't break into my Alpha's house."

"I didn't break into your Alpha's house," the Bear parroted.

Gabe shot the man a look and holstered his weapon. "How can the Halle Pride be of assistance to the Senate?" Thank God his gran had filled his head with proper etiquette, so he knew what to say even if his tone wasn't properly respectful. He'd have no clue how to deal with a Senate representative otherwise. Even if the one standing in his living room wasn't exactly the kind of person he would have expected the Senate to send.

"By giving us their Second."

Gabe blinked. He must be more tired than he thought. "Excuse me?"

"We need you to come with me."

What? No. No fucking way. He'd *just* come home after working in Philadelphia for years, gaining enough experience to take over the spot of sheriff in his beloved hometown. The town's council had been thrilled to have one of their own in the position when Adrian Giordano's father had retired. Gabe had discovered his mate only a week before, but trying to ensure that Sheri, Adrian's mate, stayed safe had eaten into all of his spare time. They'd *just* finished cleaning up after the rogue Wolf who'd been stalking Sheri and making her life a living hell. Now that he actually had time to breathe he wanted to settle down and claim his mate. No way in hell was he leaving Halle even for a minute. Not unless he could take Sarah with him.

Just thinking about sweet, tempting Sarah was enough to stiffen his resolve. Images of the dark-haired beauty had been haunting him all week. Whatever the Senate wanted they'd have to find someone else to do it. "They can't have me."

The man shook his head. "I don't think you understand, son." He headed into the kitchen like he owned it. "You need more coffee, by the way."

Gabe held back a growl. "I have a mate to claim."

The man stopped and looked back at him. "I promise you, the task I need you for will take no more than six months. After that, you'll return to Halle to live your life and claim your mate." The smile was gone. The gray eyes were somber. "We lost a Hunter, Gabriel."

"My condolences." Gabe was sincere. In a lot of ways the Hunters were the elite cops of the shifters. Their main purpose was to ensure that rogues were taken out before they could do damage to the human or shifter population. If the situation with Rudy Parker hadn't been taken care of so quickly by the Poconos Pack Alpha, Gabe would have insisted that a Hunter be called in to deal with Parker and the Wolves who followed him. He probably should have from the start. If he had, Belle Campbell would never have gotten hurt and odds were Sheri wouldn't have been kidnapped.

"Thank you. Daniel was a good friend of mine." James headed towards the kitchen again. "But that means that this region is short a Hunter."

Oh fuck. Gabe's shoulders twitched. A part of him was eager to hear more. This was like a small-town cop being picked out of the blue to become a US marshal. Another part of him wanted this man gone so he could take a shower, rest and fetch his woman home. He had plans for that sweet ass of hers, damn it. "Why me? Why not one of Rick's Wolves?" Or even another Puma, like Adrian, the current Marshal?

James smiled again. "Because they wouldn't be *you*. You're the one who's meant to be this region's new Hunter."

"I'd have to leave Halle." Gabe was surprised the words even left his mouth. He couldn't seriously be considering this.

Could he?

"Halle would be your hometown, your base of operations.

And really? Being a Hunter doesn't affect your standing in your Pride, other than you have to go when the call to hunt goes out. If that's an issue with your Alpha, and I don't think it will be, then you might have problems."

"That still doesn't answer the question." He opened the fridge and pulled out a beer. "Why me?"

"Can I have a Coke?" Gabe handed James one. "Thanks. Do you remember when you tried to shoot out the tires on Parker's car? When you figured out it was an RF jammer that was keeping Ms. Montgomery's call from reaching Dr. Giordano? And when you got the Pride together to make sure Parker and his rogues didn't get away?"

Gabe blinked, shocked. How the hell did this man know all that? "Yeah. It happened only two days ago." Two long, exhausting days ago. Gabe yawned, not caring how James took it. He was fucking *tired.*

James took a long drink from the can. "Damn, that hits the spot. You started barking orders and the Wolves and the Pumas followed them."

"So?" He belatedly twisted the cap off his beer and tossed it onto the counter.

The look James was giving him was full of amusement. "Do you think the Wolves would have listened to you if you'd merely been Marshal's Second? A *Puma* Marshal's Second?"

The bottle paused halfway to his lips. He'd sent one of the Wolves to check Max's car and sure enough they'd found a radio frequency jammer. They were highly illegal, but not impossible to make, especially for a man who'd studied electrical engineering the way Rudy Parker had. Rudy had used it to keep Sheri from contacting Adrian, convincing her that he had Adrian and luring her out of the house. The Pack Alpha, Rick, had been shot trying to protect her. Gabe had tried to stop them, but it was too late. His shot missed the getaway car's back tire and Sheri had been kidnapped.

The rogue Wolves were dead now, killed by Rick and his Pack Marshal, Ben Malone. Gabe had just finished disposing of the evidence. He was bone weary and not in any mood to deal with this shit. "I repeat. So?"

"Son, you were acting as a Hunter."

Gabe snorted and took a swig of his beer. "I was not."

"I think I know a fellow Hunter when I see one. Only a Hunter could make someone outside his species obey a direct order and *only* when hunting Rogues."

Gabe pointed at James with the beer bottle. "That's not true. An Alpha could make someone obey using their power."

James shrugged. "An Alpha's power is... different." He toyed with the tab on top of the can. "How did you know to look for the RF jammer?"

"Logic. The cell phones of all of the men were on, but not a single call got through. There had to be a reason."

"But an RF jammer? That's pretty specific."

Gabe shrugged. He was beginning to get irritated. "Look, I just *knew,* okay?"

James smiled at him like a proud papa. "Exactly."

Gabe rubbed the glass bottle across his forehead. He was getting a headache. "This makes no sense. Either you're part of the hierarchy or you're not. I'm Second. That means I'm part of the hierarchy."

James chuckled. "Is that all? Of course you're Halle's Second! That won't change."

"How could it not? You said I'd be gone for six months and when I came back I'd be a Hunter." And probably out of a job, damn it. He loved being sheriff.

"How many rogues do you think actually exist?"

"As many as there are criminals."

This time it was James who looked confused.

"The majority of the populace is law-abiding citizens. A percentage of them are not. Some places have more, some less. It would be the same with rogue shifters." He took another swig of beer and headed back into the living room. "Some of them are like the local college kids, looking for a good, illicit time. Some of them are stone-cold killers who need to be taken down."

"Daniel was taken down by a killer."

Gabe stopped. He set the beer carefully on the coffee table. He felt on edge, just like he did when he saw a really bad case cross his desk. *Fuck.* In the background the video game's music began playing again. "How?"

James picked up the remote and sat on the sofa, starting the game back up. "Want to find out?"

Yes. Damn it, yes, he did. "What about Sarah?"

James smiled. "She's your mate, Gabe. She'll still be here when we're done."

Gabe relaxed. It meant holding off on claiming his woman, but the urge to, well, *hunt* was on him. "Could this guy be a threat to Halle?"

James shook his head. "He's been killing up by Yonkers."

"New *York?*" He'd have to go to New York?

"That will be part of your territory."

Hell. New York City alone probably needed a Hunter. "How many Hunters are in this region?"

"Including you? Three. And your territory includes Pennsylvania, New York state and New Jersey."

Well hell. Add one for Atlantic City. "So I get everything

that's not New York City and Atlantic City?"

James pointed at him and crowed. "Ha! Gotcha."

Gabe realized how he'd phrased that and groaned. "Fuck." He picked up his beer and finished it. "Let me at least claim my mate."

James raised one eyebrow. "Do you really want to do that to her? Claim her and leave her for six months?" He shook his head. "Better you leave her unclaimed, for now. The mate dreams will be hell, but trust me, boy. You'll want time when you claim her." His grin turned heated. "Don't you want to be able to love on her until you're done, rather than bite her and run?"

Gabe thought of all the things he wanted to do to Sarah. The way he'd tie her to the bed, wrists bound to the headboard, eyes blindfolded. The spankings he wanted to administer to those lily-white ass cheeks, watching them turn red under his hand. He longed to feel her mouth on him, to taste her essence until he was glutted.

"I'll need to ask for a leave of absence."

"Claim family reasons." James pulled out a piece of paper. "Your maternal grandfather is ill and you need to care for him."

Gabe looked at the forged papers. His maternal grandfather had died before he'd been born. "You're kidding me, right?" He couldn't turn in forged papers. It was against the law. He handed them back to James.

James took them. "Sure. Go ahead and explain to your bosses that you're hunting a killer Wolf. Tell them that you'll be gone for roughly six months, barring holidays because we're not complete bastards, training to take up the duties of a Senate Hunter. They'll be fine with it, right?"

Gabe groaned. He just knew he was going to get fired. "Give me the damn papers."

The ringing of the phone woke her early that day. "Hello?"

"Sarah?"

She sat up, suddenly wide awake. "Gabe? Hi!" Sarah pushed her hair behind her ear, nervous as all hell. The sound of the sexy sheriff's voice was enough to have her hands shaking. She'd been waiting for his call, or expecting him to show up on her doorstep for over a week now.

The first time she'd seen the dark-haired, blue-eyed sheriff she'd rocked back on her heels, stunned. Her mate had looked equally shocked. He'd started towards her at that Pride meeting, but then Max had called for their attention and Gabe hadn't been available for more than a quick phone call since. The last time she'd seen him had been across Belle's hospital bed. He'd looked so grim she hadn't had the heart to say anything to him. He'd nodded approvingly at her before exiting the room, leaving behind a lingering warmth that had sustained her through some rough times this week.

Now that the situation with Rudy Parker was finally resolved, it was time for him to claim her.

"I need to talk to you."

His voice was serious. "Um. Okay." She bit her lip, thinking rapidly. Her stomach rumbled, reminding her she'd only had a cup of soup for dinner the night before. "Frank's Diner?"

He sighed. "I'm sorry, but I can't."

"Oh." She bit back her disappointment. At least he was speaking to her.

"I'm at the airport."

What? "Is everything all right?"

"Everything's...different."

That didn't sound good. His voice sounded weary and strained, not surprising considering what had happened a few days ago. "Different how?"

"I'm going away for a little while." She could hear the noises of an airport in the background and assumed it was Philadelphia International.

"Oh."

"Sarah. You know you're mine, right?"

Yes! "I know." She'd known the moment she'd seen him. Everything in her had yearned towards him, but she'd understood why he'd held off on claiming her. He'd needed all of his focus to be on Sheri, not Sarah. She'd been proud of him for it.

"I can't claim you yet. It's complicated. I won't be able to claim you for a while."

Her heart sank. She'd been looking forward to having someone of her own, someone who might understand some of the strange things that had been happening to her lately. "Why not?"

"I've been tapped to replace a Hunter for our region."

Pride swelled within her, along with fear. Being a Hunter was no easy job. "Oh wow. Gabe! That's...scary. Incredible, but really scary."

He laughed. "Yeah, that pretty much sums it up. Seems a rogue took one down in our area and the Senate's decided I'm the one to replace him."

"Is the Pride in danger?"

"No, baby. Halle is safe. He's operating out of New York state." The warmth in his voice went far in melting the chill that had enveloped her.

"You'll do fine, Gabe." She blinked. That hadn't been what

she'd wanted to say at all.

But it was the *right* thing to say from the relief in his tone. "I'm glad you understand, baby. This means a great deal to me, more than I thought it would when I got approached. It means when something like Parker happens again I can act without any fear of reprisals from Packs, Prides or Dens."

She settled back down on the bed. No point in getting up early on a Saturday if there was no one she had to see and nowhere to go. "How did Adrian and Max react to this? Are they all right with it?"

"Once they got away from their mates for a few seconds they were okay with it. Max actually drove me to the airport."

She stifled the hurt that he hadn't asked her to drive him. "I could have taken you."

Silence. *Not good.* "I couldn't let you do that, Sarah."

"Why not?"

"If I had been in a car with you for two hours I would never have gotten on that plane."

The rough rasp of his voice played over her senses. It was nice to know that he wanted her just as much as...she... "Where are you?"

"Right now? Somewhere near Chicago."

"Somewhere near Chicago. Not actually in Chicago." *Liar.* She just knew he was in Chicago, not that it mattered.

He gave another rough sigh. "Sarah. Please. Tell me you understand why I'm doing this."

She rubbed her hand over her eyes wearily. "I *do* understand what you're doing, but I don't like that you wouldn't even see me before you left."

"I told you why. I didn't think it was fair to either one of us to be marked before I left. I have to have my mind in the game,

123

not on my mate."

That hurt. She understood, really she did, but it still hurt. "All right."

More silence. "That's it?"

"What do you want me to say, Gabe? I understand. I don't agree, but I understand. What's going to happen the first time you go on a hunt though? Are you going to regret leaving me behind then, too?"

"I'm hoping the first time I have to go on a hunt the first flush of mating will be over and we'll be long since settled."

She thought about that for a moment. There wasn't anything more she could say about it. What was done was done. "When will you be back?"

She was beginning to hate those little silences. It meant she wasn't going to like his answer. "Six months, roughly."

She was right. She didn't like the answer. "Damn."

"I'm sorry, baby. I did what I thought was best."

She suppressed a growl. If he'd spoken to her before leaving she could have corrected that little assumption, but it was too late now. "Call me."

"I will. I promise."

January

"Shhh. Not a sound. Do you understand me?"

She nodded, her eyes lowered submissively as she knelt before him.

"Good girl." Gabe reached out and ran his hands over Sarah's soft, short hair lightly enough to cause a shudder to run through her. He smiled and tilted her chin up, loving the wary

*heat in her deep brown eyes. "You're going to do everything I tell
you to do. Aren't you?"*

*One brow rose in mild challenge before a sassy smile
crossed her full, pouty lips. He growled and tapped one finger to
his thigh, pleased when she once again lowered her eyes. Her
smile changed, becoming mysterious and feminine. It intrigued
him. Everything about her intrigued him.*

"Put your hands behind your back."

*She complied slowly. Her lashes fluttered and her breath
quickened. They'd done this before. She knew what it was he
wanted. He slipped his cock out of his uniform pants, stroking it
slowly. A groan nearly escaped his lips when she licked her own,
moistening them and making them gleam in the candlelight. He
painted her lips with the tip of his cock, the drop of pre-come
glistening there like gloss. "Open up."*

*She opened her mouth, her tongue darting out to lick just the
tip of his cock. He put his hand on the back of her head, holding
her steady as he fed her his dick. He began fucking her mouth,
losing some of his tight control and groaning at the wet heat.
"That's it, baby." She choked a bit and he backed off a little,
proud of her for holding steady despite it.*

*He was close, so close, but he didn't want to come in her
mouth. Not tonight. Tonight he wanted that sweet, hot pussy
wrapped around him, pulling his orgasm out of him.*

*He withdrew from her mouth, stroking her hair as she
pouted up at him. "Stand up." She complied, lowering her eyes
once more, her hands still behind her back. "Lie down on the
bed."*

*She looked up at him, startled. He lifted his chin, pointing to
the big, dark bed right behind her. He didn't understand how she
could have missed it. It dominated the room they were in.*

She crawled onto the bed on all fours, giving him an amazing view of that incredible ass of hers. He halted her, hands on her hips, and nipped one of her white globes, loving the shiver that ran through her. He slapped her lightly on the ass, smiling wickedly as a pink mark rose up. "Middle of the bed, on your back."

She moved the way he directed, settling down with a final shimmy that caused her breasts to dance.

"Spread your arms and legs." She bit her lip but complied, slowly showing him the liquid heat between her thighs.

He reached down and tied each one of her limbs, careful to make sure none of the bindings were too tight on her slender frame. When he was done, he looked at her, knowing exactly what the feral look on his face would do to her.

He watched as she swallowed nervously. She tugged at the restraints, testing them.

He began a slow exploration of her body, stroking her soft flesh until goose bumps rose on her skin. He licked at her pert nipples, watching her squirm under him. When he sucked her clit into his mouth she bucked against him. She was lucky he hadn't told her to hold still, or that would have earned her a spanking.

He could hear her gasping for breath and he knew she was close to coming. He slid up her body, thrusting inside her so hard she whimpered.

He grinned. "That's two."

Her golden eyes went wide. It was the hottest fucking thing he'd ever seen, watching her dark eyes turn tawny. She always managed to hold off the change until he was fucking her, letting him watch it happen while he was deep inside her body. He was proud at the measure of control it took to keep the Puma at bay for that long, while at the same time he was desperate to break it. "Keep your eyes open." Her lids drooped in a sensuous daze but didn't close as he pounded into her. She kept her gaze locked on his, her arms and legs struggling futilely against the bonds he had her in. He reached down, stroking her clit with his thumb, snarling in triumph as she screeched. He leaned over her, whispering in her ear. "That's three." Her body bowed up, quivering at the force of her orgasm.

She nipped his earlobe as her body settled back onto the mattress and he came, the pleasure so intense it robbed him of breath. He collapsed on top of her, his cheek resting against hers, his whiskers abrading her sleek skin.

One salty tear wound down her cheek to fall against his. "Where are you?"

He lifted his head. Sorrow filled her face, his heart nearly ripping in two at the sight. "Sarah. Baby."

Gabe woke up sweating and horny as all hell. He started to whip the sleeping bag open but remembered in time that he was in a tent in the middle of a snowy field. *Fuck.* If it wasn't for the fact that so far he loved what he was doing, this job would suck. Part of him wished he'd told James to fuck off and claimed Sarah the way he'd wanted to. The other part knew James was probably right, that it would have been ten times worse to taste Sarah and leave her behind.

He punched his pillow and prayed he'd be able to sleep without any more dreams. James snored beside him, loud enough to rattle the insulated cloth. *If I get back to sleep at all.*

After about twenty minutes he gave up. Stripping quickly, he unzipped the tent and slipped out into the night. It was fucking cold, but it wouldn't be for much longer. Shivering, he zipped the tent back up and made sure it was secure before he shifted and allowed his Puma out to run.

His paws dug into the snow, the cold air rushing past his whiskers. It felt glorious to let his Puma out without the presence of the Bear who was training him. He'd have to go back all too soon, but for now he'd allow the night air to wash the dreams of his Sarah away.

Chapter Two

March

Gabe shivered and pulled off his parka. Damn, this last hunting lesson had been harsh. He wasn't certain he'd ever feel his toes again. "I'm going to call Max, let him know how things are going."

James waved, hanging up his cowboy hat and heading towards the kitchen of his three-bedroom cabin. He'd promised Gabe a nice thick stew in return for learning snow tracking.

Gabe hung up the parka and pulled off his snow-encrusted boots, leaving them on the mat by the door. It had become routine in the last three months. James hated wet floors. The last time Gabe had forgotten to leave his boots on the mat he'd found them in his bed, snow and all.

He pulled out his cell phone and dialed Max. "Hey, Max."

"Gabe! How's it going out in the Montana wilderness?"

"Fucking cold. How're things in Halle?" *How's Sarah?*

"Fucking cold."

Gabe snorted. "I'm learning some new tracking techniques." He'd need them in the winter months in New York. He'd be heading there soon with James to spend a couple of weeks. So far he'd been all over the territory he'd be protecting, learning the land in a way only a solitary shifter could. He'd never know it as well as a native, but he'd be able to track the different terrains he'd be dealing with. He'd met the other two Hunters, a young Fox named Desiree Holt and an older Coyote named Edmund Graves. Both had interesting insights into the areas where they lived. Desiree lived in New Jersey; Graves lived in New York City. Gabe had been surprised when he heard that. Coyotes and Wolves didn't get along very well. To learn there was a Coyote Pack that close to Rick's Wolves had startled him. Afterwards James had taken him back to his home in Montana to learn what he called "*real* snow tracking".

Gabe's responsibility would mostly be to the Pennsylvania area, but he'd be called to assist the others whenever needed and vice versa. With luck he'd never need to.

Daniel, the Hunter who'd been killed, had also been a Fox and a friend of Desiree's. She'd been instrumental in bringing the rogue who'd killed him to justice.

"I even have the secret handshake now." The amused snort from the kitchen let him know James could hear everything. "I can call in the other Hunters if someone like Rudy ever shows his snout in Halle again." The growl from the other room reminded him of his place. "Or anywhere else in Pennsylvania."

"Good. Adrian and Sheri want you to call them, by the way."

"Will do." He didn't know them well enough to miss them yet, but he and Adrian had developed a rapport that would only grow stronger with time. Before too long he expected his relationship with Adrian would be similar to the one Max shared with Simon, his Beta.

"And Emma says bring her back something, but make sure it doesn't have antlers or fur."

Gabe laughed. Emma was a riot. "Taken care of." He'd already packed a Kachina doll for the Curana in his luggage for when he returned to Halle. He'd picked it up in Arizona, the current seat of the Senate. "How's Sarah?"

Max sighed. "I'm not sure. She knows what you're doing, but I think she'd feel better if you'd call her and talk to her."

"I have." Many times. Sarah understood what he was doing but was hurt when he wouldn't tell her where he was. He couldn't, by shifter law, tell her where he was while he was in Arizona. The Senate's compound was highly restricted. Only those on Senate business were allowed in or out. Sarah wouldn't have been able to be with him there even if she knew where it was. Knowing that had eased some of it, but her frustration was slowly building. He could hear it in her voice every time he spoke to her.

Then he'd been sent to help hunt down the rogue in New York. He hadn't been able to call until the man was captured and brought to justice. He'd proven to himself that he really did have what it took to be a Hunter. The pride he'd felt at his accomplishment had spilled over when he'd gotten hold of his mate afterwards. Even so, he'd kept to what James had told him, calling Sarah only after he'd left the area. If he'd seen her he'd have claimed her. After all these months of mate dreams nothing would have stopped him.

The one time he'd managed to get an entire week in Halle she hadn't even been there. She'd made other plans for the holidays, assuming that he'd be too busy to make the trip to Halle. They'd both been upset by that. If he'd known she'd made other plans he would have told her a lot sooner that he was coming to visit. Hell, who was he kidding? He'd had every intention of marking her ass before an hour in Halle had passed. But he'd decided to surprise her, and instead the surprise was on him when she wasn't even there.

As for James's house, the Bear had refused to allow her to

come, saying that she'd be a major distraction for Gabe, who was still in training. He'd compared it to boot camp, saying wives weren't allowed until after it was over.

But boot camp only lasted eight weeks, a complaint James had waved off. And to be honest, he was usually too exhausted to do more than eat or sleep. James was working him harder than he'd ever worked before. They'd spent days out in the snow, tracking different shifter volunteers from the Senate. He could track Fox, Coyote, Wolf and Puma now. In fact they'd just come back from one such excursion. The only ones they hadn't practiced with were Lion, Tiger, Lynx and Jaguar, but James assured him they were up next.

It killed Gabe to tell Sarah that, no, she couldn't come visit. She'd been answering her phone less and less, and he'd taken to calling less and less. When they did manage to get in contact with one another their conversations tended to end in stony silence. The only thing that eased his mind was his rapidly growing friendship with the little red-haired waitress from Frank's Diner. The Fox had offered to keep an eye on his mate in exchange for his help in moving her family to Halle. She'd become a good friend, almost the little sister he'd never had. She was bubbly and happy most of the time, and loved the work she was doing just as much as he did.

But the mate dreams were killing him. *Killing. Him.* If she was willing to do half of what he dreamed of he'd be one happy cat.

Hell, even if she never chose to allow him to indulge his darker side he'd be one happy cat. Still, he hoped to talk her into a few things. Watching her come in his dreams, tied to his bed, blindfolded and begging, couldn't compare to seeing it for real.

"I'll call her tonight. I promise." And she'd better answer.

He was tired of talking to a machine.

Sarah Parker heard the phone ring and ran for it. One of the bags of groceries slipped, spilling soda all over her floor. "Damn." She'd have to wait a day to drink that.

"Hi, this is Sarah. Leave a message after the beep." *Beep.*

"Sarah, it's Gabe." A resigned sigh gusted out of the speaker. "Call me."

Sarah grabbed the receiver. "Hello!" But he'd already hung up. "Double damn." He'd sounded so tired. She dialed him back, but his line was busy. She left a message, hoping he'd call her back that night, but knowing that he wouldn't. He never did.

She knew what he was doing was important. She wasn't selfish enough to keep him from that. But why couldn't he have mated her *before* he left? Things would have been so much easier. For one thing the fact that she got to hear more about what was going on in his life from fucking Chloe Williams, aka Super Waitress, wouldn't bother her quite so much. He managed to talk to the redhead way more than he did Sarah, and it was really beginning to bug the shit out of her.

What *really* sucked was the fact that he'd managed to get home for Christmas. Unfortunately Sarah hadn't known he was coming, so she'd made plans to visit her family in Florida. She'd left the day before Gabe arrived in Halle, much to their mutual annoyance.

She heard he'd spent a nice time with Chloe. He'd bought the other woman a pretty little charm bracelet with tiny cats and foxes on it. Sarah had to hold back a growl every time she saw it. If it wasn't for the fact that she'd struck up a friendship with Jim Woods she'd have lost her mind long ago.

The handsome veterinarian was a lifeline for her. They went

everywhere together, had a good time together. He knew all about her love for Gabe and accepted the fact that he'd never get any further than friendship, so the tension that usually came with a new relationship wasn't even there. He was funny, he was kind to animals, and he'd grown up in the area so he knew almost everyone. They had a blast together. He was even Emma's ex-boyfriend, but somehow he'd managed to make friends with Max, something Sarah hadn't thought possible considering how territorial the Alpha was towards his mate.

She'd met him at Max and Emma's, in fact. He'd been there when she'd gone over to discuss a new development with Max, something that had scared the crap out of her at the time. She hadn't understood what was happening to her at first, but Max had managed to help her sort out what was wrong, and Emma had introduced her to Jim.

But Jim wasn't Gabe. He never could be. And she was missing her mate more and more with each passing day. The mate dreams were shocking, explicit, and left her damp and wrung out. The marks on her body were a constant reminder of what awaited her once Gabe got over his training and came home to claim her.

If he claimed her. She was slowly beginning to have doubts about that. He'd spent an *awful* lot of time talking to another woman for Sarah to feel upbeat about their future mating.

She tried one more time to call Gabe back, but got his voicemail. "Gabe, it's Sarah. I was bringing in groceries and missed your call. Call me back, okay? I have something to tell you." She sighed, grabbing the mop out of the closet. "I miss you." She hung up and began to clean up the spilled cola.

"So will Gabe be back in time for the wedding?" Jim picked up his French fry and dipped it in some ketchup.

"I have no idea. I haven't spoken to him in about two weeks." Her nerves were completely frazzled. The last time she'd heard his voice had been on her answering machine. He'd never called her back, never heard her news.

This long-distance crap really sucked. If it wasn't for the fact that she *knew* he was alive she'd be much more upset. Not that she wasn't thinking of killing him when she finally did get hold of him.

"Tell you what, if he's not back in time we can go together."

She smiled at Jim. God, he was so nice. Jim Woods felt...sweet. Safe. Like a man you could rely on no matter what. But deep down, there was a small spark of mischief in him that would be irresistible to the right woman, and a core of strength that would shock anyone who took him at face value. All of that was wrapped up in a package that screamed all-American hometown boy-next-door. Blond and hazel-eyed, he stood a full head taller than she. He wasn't as broad-shouldered as Gabe, his legs not as muscular, but his grin was engaging in ways not even Gabe could manage. He was a treat to all of her senses. If she hadn't been so hung up on her mate she'd have made a move on him a long time ago. "Wouldn't you rather bring a *real* date?"

His expression was charming and open, but that little mischievous spark danced in his eyes. "Think of the fun we could have!" He shrugged. "Besides, you know I'm not interested in dating right now."

Liar. She had a good idea of exactly who he'd like to be dating, and it wasn't her. "You should ask her out." It would certainly make Sarah feel better if he asked out the woman he really wanted.

He made a face. "She's too young for me."

She tried not to eye the bouncing red ponytail of Chloe

Williams. "She's not *that* young."

"She's twenty-two."

"Yup. And you're an ancient, wrinkled mess."

He almost choked on his French fry.

A new iced tea landed in front of her. "Can I get you anything else?"

Sarah held back her sigh. For some reason Chloe seemed to be pissed at her today. "Nope. Thanks."

"Oh hey, I heard from Gabe last night. He said to tell you hello."

Sarah gritted her teeth. "Thanks." The sympathy in Jim's gaze was almost too much to bear. "That will be all, Chloe."

Chloe hesitated for a moment. "Right. Should I tell him to give you a call tonight?"

He's calling her again tonight? He talked to Chloe almost every day, but couldn't be bothered to call his mate. Sarah's temper, normally hard to rouse, snapped its leash. "Don't bother."

Chloe looked like she wanted to say something more, a frown marring the smooth surface of her skin, but Sarah chose to ignore it. "All right. Holler if you need anything."

Sarah ignored the other woman, focusing instead on her nearly empty plate. The burger sat in her stomach like lead.

"So. Want to be my wedding date?"

Sarah looked up into Jim's warm hazel eyes. "Sure." After all, it looked like her mate wouldn't care one way or the other. But first she was going to make a little appointment with Dr. Howard. She was tired of dreaming about something it looked like she was never going to have.

Chapter Three

April

Oh my God. Sarah gaped at the sight of Gabriel Anderson standing in the Philadelphia Airport. He looked so tired it broke her heart. She took a step towards him, her heart hammering in joy and disbelief.

He's home.

"Gabe!" A flash of red streaked past her. Gabe looked startled for a moment but smiled and held out his arms. Chloe jumped into them, wrapping her legs around the sheriff's waist.

Gabe's face was slowly turning red, but the affection pouring off him for the woman in his arms twisted through Sarah's gut. "Um. Hello, vixen."

Next to her Jim cleared his throat. "Sorry, kiddo. Looks like lover-boy has a girlfriend."

Sarah opened up just enough to feel the hurt Jim was trying to hide, then slammed her shields back into place. She'd gotten good at building those shields in the last few months. She was tired of other people's pity hammering into her recently. Even with Jim pity flavored his pain. "This is all your fault."

"My fault? How is this my fault?"

She turned to him with a grin. "Because you never asked

her out, Dr. Jurassic."

He made a face. "Sure, blame everything on me." He took hold of her arm and led her towards the gate. "We're sitting together, right?"

She heard Gabe calling her name but ignored him. "Sure are."

"Because neither one of us wants to watch the two of them together."

She grimaced. "Right. Hey, maybe they'll be so busy saying hello they'll forget to get on the plane!"

They headed down the ramp, arms entwined. "You always see the bright side. That's what I love about you."

She giggled. At the very least, Jim would keep her entertained, despite her heartbreak. She couldn't even bring herself to look at Gabe.

He'd made his choice clear. And it wasn't her.

"Is everything okay?"

Gabe looked down at Chloe. She was normally good company, but today Gabe just couldn't get into a conversation with her. "Everything's fine, little vixen."

Liar, his Puma purred.

He had to admit his Puma was right. Things were far from fine. Some guy named Jim, Sarah's fucking *date* for the wedding, had her giggling like a schoolgirl as he told her some outrageous tale of his travels. Jim had been at the airport with her, smiling and obviously happy to be with her. He'd held her hand, kissing the back of it and smiling down at her seductively. He was delighted with her, commandeering her to sit next to him on the plane, tucking her hand into the crook of his arm, even carrying her luggage. And when Sarah had tripped, Jim had caught her, saving her from a nasty fall. He'd even planted a soft kiss on Sarah's forehead.

Gabe had wanted to break Jim's pretty-boy face at the sight of the other man's hands around her waist, his lips on her skin. His Puma was growling so loudly Gabe was surprised his chest wasn't vibrating.

And Jim *was* pretty. Even as a guy Gabe could see that. He had that smarmy charm women seemed to fall all over themselves for.

Sarah certainly didn't seem immune to it. Jim reached up and brushed some of that golden hair off his forehead and half the females on the plane sighed, including Sarah.

He stared at Sarah, torn. *Why was she acting like this?* He'd gotten straight off the plane, exhausted from making sure he was back in Philadelphia in time to go to the wedding of his Alpha and Curana, only to find his mate hanging all over another man. He couldn't have imagined the shocked joy on her face when she'd first caught sight of him, but he'd been distracted by Chloe's overenthusiastic greeting. Once he'd gotten himself disentangled from his friend, Sarah had latched onto Jimbo. She'd barely acknowledged he was there. A growl escaped his control when Jim stroked Sarah's soft cheek. *Oh, fucker. Get your hands off her or I'm gonna eat 'em.* He saw Jim's gaze travel down to where Sarah's little flowered sundress revealed the sweet swell of her breasts and wanted to rip the bastard's eyes out of his head.

Gabe forcibly kept the snarl off his face but was helpless to stop his eyes from changing. She'd touched him. She'd dragged those delicate fingers of hers down Jim's arm, her expression full of mischief and admiration.

Gabe didn't like that. Not one damn bit. Jealousy churned

in his gut. He wanted to pounce on the other man and rip his goddamn throat out for putting that soft look on his mate's face.

But what startled him was the sound Chloe made as she watched the couple down the aisle having a wonderful time together. The moment Jim's hand touched Sarah, an odd, high-pitched yip left her lips. She clamped her mouth shut immediately, turning her face away from the couple to stare at the seat in front of her. Her cheeks turned bright red and she refused to look at anyone. She blew her bangs out of her face, a gesture that reminded him of Sarah. He glanced over at his mate to see her leaning her head against Jim's shoulder.

"You shouldn't have left."

Gabe's hands clenched in his lap. He would *not* get up and throw the fucker off the plane. He. Would. *Not.* "You know why I had to. Hell, *she* knows why I had to."

"Then why don't you go over there and do something about it?"

Gabe gritted his teeth. He'd like nothing better than to get his hands on Sarah right now. He hadn't spoken to her since March, and Chloe's updates on his mate's whereabouts had been less than encouraging. She seemed to spend an awful lot of time with the handsome veterinarian. Hell, he'd gotten so upset he'd cut his training short by a week just to be with her.

What the hell is she thinking? She had to know how he'd feel about her touching someone else, especially after being apart for so long. He'd meant to see to it that they were mated this week. Now that his training was finally over he was home to stay. But instead of being thrilled to see him she'd frowned and turned her fucking back on him.

He couldn't remember anything that had hurt him more. Or pissed him off more. Her ass was going to be very sore by the time the week was over.

"While you sit there with your thumb up your stubborn kitty ass *my* mate is making goo-goo eyes at *your* mate."

His head whipped around to study Chloe. "So why don't *you* go over there and do something?"

She flushed. "He thinks I'm a kid. I overheard him telling someone at the office."

The low, canine growl in her voice nearly matched the feline one lodged in his throat. "Well I hope you're one of those people who have more than one mate, because I'm gonna kill me a vet if he doesn't learn to keep his hands to himself."

Chloe glared at him. "And what should I do about your sweet little pus—"

He slapped his hand over her mouth. "Don't call her that. It's not polite."

She grumbled against his palm. He laughed, ignoring the looks the other passengers sent their way.

He also tried to ignore the niggling little voice telling him that maybe Chloe was right. That maybe he *had* made a mistake he was now paying for. It should have been his hands stroking Sarah's satiny skin, not Jim's. But what in hell was he supposed to do about it now? He sat back and stared out the plane's window. He had no idea what to do, but he knew he had to stop watching Sarah and Jim. If he didn't, there'd be an animal-related death at thirty thousand feet.

Sarah tried to ignore how happy Gabe and Chloe seemed as they left Orlando International Airport. Their heads were close together, deep in conversation as they waited for their luggage.

Sarah was still in shock. She hadn't known Gabe would be

able to make the trip to Florida. It wasn't like he bothered to call her and tell her his plans anymore. Sarah tried to hear what they were talking about, but the noisy Orlando airport was just too much. Jim stayed close by her side, trying his best to keep her spirits up in the face of Chloe and Gabe's obvious involvement.

The affection she could feel pouring off Gabe every time he looked at Chloe was tearing her apart.

"Emma says I'm riding in the limo with you, but Chloe isn't."

Ouch. "Won't she be offended?"

Jim grinned down at her, putting the last of their bags on the cart. "Do you really care?"

She didn't even have to think about it. "Nope. Do you care?"

Jim laughed, gaining both Gabe's and Chloe's attention. They both glared at Jim, though why Chloe would be angry with the man Sarah had no clue. Jim, the big ham, leaned down and bussed her cheek. "They're watching us."

"Mm-hmm."

Jim surprised her, picking her up and twirling her away from the baggage return. She squealed, laughing when he put her down. "Having fun, sweetheart?"

She nodded up at him, grinning like a loon.

She tried to ignore it when Gabe helped Chloe get her rental car, joining them at the limo only once he was sure she was on her way. There was only so much distraction Jim could provide.

"Everyone ready?" Max gently ushered Emma inside the limo, his gaze lingering on his mate's pert backside. He settled next to Emma and had her in his lap within seconds. Emma curled around him, sighing softly.

Sarah climbed in next, delighted when Jim sat next to her. She immediately snuggled closer to him, giving Adrian and Sheri, the Pride Marshall and his mate, room to get in. Dr. Adrian Giordano was Max's business partner; his pale, legally blind mate was the latest addition to the Halle Pride.

Rick and Belle, the Poconos Pack Alphas, took the seat next to the door. The large Pack Alpha settled Belle in with unexpected gentleness, careful of the hip she'd injured saving Sheri from her insane ex-boyfriend. Her hip was better now, but thanks to a rival, Belle had been forced to have the pins removed too soon in order to shift and face a dominance challenge. She'd limp for the rest of her life because of it, but Rick didn't seem to care. They'd both been asked to be in the wedding, an honor they'd accepted happily. Rick's long red hair was pulled back in a tail, wisps flying up in the Florida breeze as he climbed in after his petite Luna.

"Damn, Rick. You need to wash your hair." Simon, the Pride Beta and Max's best man, climbed in, pretending to spit out bits of the Wolf's hair. Becky, Emma's Beta and matron of honor, climbed in after him, laughing and smacking Simon on the arm as Rick gave Simon the one-finger salute.

Gabe was the last party member in the limo. He stopped short when he saw Sarah sitting close to Jim, his gaze fixed on the hand Jim had resting on her thigh.

Sarah turned her face away from Gabe, looking up at Jim with affection. The entire plane ride Gabe had chatted and laughed with Chloe, showing no signs that Sarah's sitting with Jim bothered him in the least.

So why is he growling?

She used her newfound powers to try and figure out how Gabe felt and was shocked. He was livid. Jim looked remarkably like a chew toy to the Second.

Jim leaned down, his gaze caressing her face as his fingers stroked her thigh. "So, how about dinner tonight?"

"Sorry, she's busy."

She blinked, anger stirring at Gabe's smug expression. "Excuse me?" *He hasn't bothered to call me for a month and suddenly thinks he has the right to dictate my life?*

I don't think so.

"Gabe's right, Sarah." Emma shrugged, the traitor. "Tonight we've got reservations for the entire wedding party, plus Jim and Chloe, of course, at The Rainforest Café."

"Oh." She grinned up at Jim, delighted when Gabe's expression turned fierce. *Suck it up, big guy, just like I've had to every time Chloe throws your "friendship" in my face.* She knew it wasn't logical, but a tiny spurt of hope bloomed with that look. Maybe things weren't as grim as she'd thought they were. "Looks like you're taking me to dinner on Max's dime."

Everyone except Gabe chuckled.

"Tell you what. I'll take you dancing on *my* dime after dinner." Jim picked up her hand and kissed the palm, oblivious to the way Gabe's sapphire blue eyes turned gold before they were quickly shielded by his ridiculously long lashes.

"Oh, dancing! That's a great idea!" Emma giggled, her gaze darting back and forth between Gabe, Jim and Sarah.

Subtlety, thy name is not Emma. The Curana knew that Gabe and Sarah were meant to be mates and was obviously trying to play matchmaker.

Jim lifted his lips from her palm. "Does anyone hear a tearing sound?"

Sarah looked over at Gabe, not surprised to see his hands in his lap. Next to his right leg, four long furrows had been dug into the leather seat.

She tried to hide her glee at the sight. *He's actually jealous. Maybe this will work out!* She snuggled next to Jim, a small smile on her face as she listened to her friends chatting and laughing together. Only Gabe remained silent, his face cold as he watched Jim play with her fingers.

Gabe settled into his hotel room with an angry growl.

Sarah was pulling away from him.

All during the flight from Philadelphia to Orlando, he'd watched her. Not once had she glanced over to see what he was up to.

And that chapped his ass more than he thought it would. Almost as much as the fact that the mate dreams had stopped seemed to bother his Puma. He hadn't had a taste of his sweet Sarah for weeks. He had no idea what that meant, but his Puma had damn near gone into mourning.

Fuck.

He'd nearly lost it in the limo at the sight of another man's hands all over *his* mate. The only thing stopping him from changing and killing the son of a bitch had been the presence of his Pride leaders, and the fact that the very human Jim didn't stand a chance against him.

If Jim were a shifter, however, Gabe wouldn't have been able to hold back. There'd be one less dickhead in the world sniffing after his Sarah, Chloe's intended mate or not.

He lay down, intent on taking a short nap before his shower, hoping it would ease the growing headache that always seemed to be present these days. He was dreading what was going to happen at dinner. If Jim touched Sarah's soft skin one more time, he was going head first into the mouth of an animatronic gorilla.

"Sarah."

She shivered as that deep voice rolled over her. She didn't dare look up, knowing that would earn her a spanking. Not normally a bad thing, but that wasn't what she wanted just then. I wish I'd taken another one of those damn sleeping pills. She slept like the dead when she did, not dreaming at all, not even the silly little dreams she'd had before she'd met Gabe. Unfortunately she'd decided not to, not wanting to be light-headed through dinner. The sleeping pills always made her groggy when she woke up too soon. Besides, Gabe didn't seem the type to take an afternoon nap.

Admit it. Part of you thought he'd be in Chloe's room.

She gritted her teeth at the thought of him with the redhead. It made her even more determined than ever that he wouldn't get what he wanted easily. Not this time.

"Look at me, Sarah."

She peeked up at him through her lashes, allowing her defiance to shine through.

"That's one, baby. Now look up at me."

Fuck it. She would not submit. As far as she was concerned he'd betrayed her. He no longer had her obedience. He'd have to earn it back along with her trust.

"Put your hands behind your back, baby."

Sarah stubbornly kept them where they were, in her lap.

He studied her, circling her, his stride sleek and commanding. "I said, put your hands behind your back."

"No."

He stopped, one brow rising arrogantly. "No?"

She turned her face from him, the first time she'd dared to do that in their dreams.

He crouched down, one hand going to her chin, pulling her face around. She closed her eyes, refusing to look at him. "Sarah."

She opened her eyes, hoping he would see the anger and the pain. She wanted him to know what he'd done to her. "You no longer have me."

He reared back, his hand dropping from her face. Anguish flitted briefly across his face before anger washed over it. "Jim."

"Chloe." She glared at him. "Apparently she's the one who should be here right now."

"What?"

"Are you sleeping with her?"

For one second he looked stunned, confused, before determination settled in. He grabbed her upper arms, pulling her into his body. "I am not sleeping with Chloe!"

"Bullshit."

His expression turned cold. "That's two."

"That's none! How could you?"

She gasped as his eyes turned to gold. "I give you my word I have not slept with Chloe."

She turned her face away. He'd been home over Christmas, given Chloe that pretty little bracelet. He'd had the time and probably the inclination. "Liar."

Out of the corner of her eye she saw his jaw clench. "That's three."

Uh-oh. He had a hard and fast rule: three strikes, and she was out.

She fought him as he pulled her over his knee, but he was too strong for her.

"One: I have never, ever lied to you. Not even in dreams."

SMACK. His palm landed, stinging her backside. She howled, trying to pull away from him, but he held her down firmly. The sting faded quickly, her arousal growing as she tried to squirm off his lap.

"Two. I have not slept with Chloe."

Smack. This one was not as hard as the first. He caressed the mark his hand left behind. She licked her lips as her belly flipped. Normally, she loved it when he spanked her. The heat of his hand, the sting of his palm, would give way to an arousal so intense he didn't need to do anything else to get her off.

Which was why she needed to get away. She wriggled harder, pinching his thigh, trying to get him to let her go. If that third smack landed...

SMACK!

She shuddered. Licking her lips, she looked up at him through her bangs and wondered what he would do if she just sank her fangs into his leg.

"If you so much as let Jim touch your little pinky, you won't sit down for a week. Do you understand me?"

She blew a raspberry at him. He was so stunned she actually got free.

Unfortunately, it didn't last long. "Oh, no you don't." Hard arms wrapped around her, holding her against him, back to front. "A little something to remind you to be a good girl, other than your sore ass." He bit her neck, and she just knew he was sucking up a mark. If he'd let his fangs drop he'd have been marking her as his. One hand drifted down to her dripping pussy, pushing up against her clit, stroking her fast and furious until she was writhing in his embrace.

She screeched as she came, but it felt empty somehow.

With one final smack on her ass he set her free. "Now..."

Sarah woke, grateful the alarm clock had kept the dream from going any further. She just knew what he'd had in mind. Another quick, hard fuck followed by yet more rejection. With a sigh she stood and headed into the shower, stripping as she went. She was still tired. The nap had hardly been what she'd call *restful. Damn him, anyway.*

She washed quickly and toweled off, pulling her underwear out of the drawer. She didn't have much time, thanks to Gabe's little game. If she had her way, the games would stop one way or another before the end of this trip.

She wanted her hair and makeup to be perfect tonight, so she'd need to hurry. She had to do her damndest to outshine the perky female who had her mate's undivided attention. Dinner was in under an hour and she still needed to catch the shuttle to Animal Kingdom.

She dressed quickly in the strappy little red sundress and matching sandals, plugged in her blow-dryer, and began taking care of her short bob, curling the ends under to frame her face. Just as she lifted her brush she noticed the bite mark on her neck. She turned the dryer off and leaned in closer to get a better look.

"Rat bastard." It wasn't the first time he'd marked her in a dream. Light hand prints had shown up more than once on her backside, hickeys on her shoulder blades and breasts, and now this. It was nice and dark too, and right where anyone could see it. The first time it had happened she'd been freaked out. Now, she was just annoyed.

It took her a while, but she finally got it covered with

makeup. *How do I explain to people a dream hickey, anyway?*

Shaking her head she started the dryer up again. If she didn't hurry she'd be late, and it would all be Gabe's fault.

It rained of course. What else could you expect in Florida in April? Hell, at least it had helped get rid of the unfulfilled hard-on he'd been sporting since his dream of Sarah had been interrupted. He didn't even have the heart to be pissed about the aborted dream; seeing her there had been more than worth it. His Puma was actually growly again, something he hadn't thought he'd miss until it was gone. He got to the restaurant before the worst of the rain hit, so he wasn't too soaked. Still, the damp clothing and the cold air-conditioning was sending shivers down his spine and pulling up goose bumps on his arms.

He thought he was the first one there until he spied Emma shopping. The Rainforest Café was set up so that one entered the restaurant through the gift shop attached to it. He smiled as he caught Max's wince, but Emma's laughter pulled her mate to her like a magnet to iron.

He watched them, so happy together, and wondered if he and Sarah would ever be that happy. The dream this afternoon had disturbed him on more than one level. Sarah's defiance had startled him, turned him on and hurt him, all at the same time. Her pain had struck him deep, made him question his decisions like never before, even more than seeing her with Jim had. The only thing he could come up with was that his Puma was bound and determined to have him finally claim her as his own.

Even in dreams she'd never argued with him like that before. He'd been telling dream-Sarah the truth. He couldn't bring himself to lie to her, even there. He *hadn't* slept with

Chloe. He hadn't been with a real woman in a long time. Hell, even his dreams were faithful to her! How could she think for even a second that he would betray their bond that way? The pain in her eyes had been too much for him to bear, and when she'd told him he didn't have her any longer, he'd nearly broken down and ended his torment, marking her for all to see as his, if only in his own mind.

He had to stop this. He had to remember that they were *only* dreams, or that pain he'd seen in her would drive him mad.

Why had his dream of her accused him of infidelity? That *really* bothered him. Was he secretly attracted to Chloe? He tried to picture kissing her and shuddered in revulsion.

Nope. That isn't it. The thought of touching any female flesh but Sarah's was revolting. *So why did Dream Sarah accuse me of that?* What was his subconscious trying to tell him? Could his closeness with Chloe be the root of his problems with Sarah? But why?

He shook his head and wondered what Sarah's dreams were like. How did he act in them? Did he bring her flowers and candy? Did he make sweet, gentle love to her? Did they argue constantly? One thing was for sure. He very much doubted he spanked her until she came.

He stopped, stunned by a single, horrifying thought. *What if she doesn't dream of me at all?*

He heard Sarah's tinkling laughter and turned towards the entrance of the restaurant, compelled to catch a glimpse of her. She was shaking water out of her hair, giggling up at the walking dead man beside her. She was soaked through, her short red sundress clinging to her curves in a way guaranteed to raise the blood pressure of any male who wasn't gay, showing off legs Gabe had felt wrapped around his waist more than once. Gabe stepped forward, instinctively looking for a way to shield his mate from other men's eyes.

Before he could reach her Jim led her right over to the towels and began gently drying her off. "Don't worry about it, sweetheart, I'll just buy it for you."

"Thank you, Jim." She gazed up at the soon-to-be corpse with affection. Affection that rightfully belonged to *him*. When Jim's towel-covered hands drifted dangerously close to her cleavage Gabe snarled, unable to hold himself back a second longer.

That's it. Dickhead's gonna find out what that towel tastes like.

The towel lifted just enough to reveal the side of Sarah's neck, halting Gabe in his tracks. His entire being was focused on the mark on her neck.

The mark he'd put there not two hours before.

He stared at it, wondering what the fuck was going on. How the hell was that possible? He hadn't actually bitten her! It had been a fucking dream, for God's sake!

She caught him staring at her. Her expression turned wary, and her hand moved up to cover the mark.

He caught her gaze with his own, trapping her, mentally demanding answers she couldn't possibly give him.

When her eyes lowered submissively, he nearly cursed out loud. His cock twitched, his erection growing to painful proportions behind his jeans despite their cold dampness.

She'd somehow been there in his dreams, in his arms, writhing on his cock, every damn night for *months*. And she'd done *everything he'd asked of her.*

She blushed, pulling back, away from him and closer to the man who was going to become cat chow.

Gabe felt the purr of his Puma, a feral sound, one that he'd become familiar with over the last few months. *Oh, hell no, baby. You can try to run, but I will hunt you down. And when I do I'm going to have a few things to say about your relationship with Dr. Deadman.*

You're mine.

Chapter Four

Gabe was watching her with obvious irritation as she settled in next to Jim, his growl of disapproval so low only the other shifters could hear him. The one time she'd dared glance at him, he'd smiled that sexier-than-hell grin of his, the one she'd seen only in her dreams, and held up one finger. She could almost hear him in her head.

That's one.

He virtually ignored Chloe, who wavered between sending him questioning looks and smiling sweetly at Jim, who in turn ignored her in favor of Sarah.

This weird love triangle was beginning to look suspiciously like a rectangle. Gabe wanted Chloe (and Sarah, if the glare he kept steadily on Jim was any indication). Sarah wanted Gabe, Chloe wanted Gabe (and Jim, from the lustful looks she kept sending his way). Jim wanted...Emma? Maybe? The vibe she got off the vet was strange. He watched Emma when he thought she wasn't looking with a sort of wistful regret, but when he looked at Chloe, he felt guilt, and enough hot lust to melt paint off the space shuttle. He really needed to get over the fact that Chloe was only twenty-two and just make a move on her. *If Gabe lets him, that is.* Because despite his glare at Jim he'd seated Chloe next to him with a gentle smile he hadn't bothered to give his mate.

She sighed and took another sip of her margarita. *A love hexagon just doesn't have the same ring to it somehow.* She needed a distraction or she was going to wind up with a migraine from all the tension at the table. Luckily it wasn't hard to be distracted in a restaurant like The Rainforest Café. Every few minutes the "animals" would squeal, squeak, roar or shout. It was hard to hear yourself think, let alone make conversation with someone else, but she and Jim managed it, mostly by leaning into each other and yelling in each others' ears.

If it wasn't for Gabe and Chloe glaring at the two of them it would have been a lot of fun.

"I think lover-boy is pissed at me," Jim shouted discreetly in her ear over the "thunderstorm". "He looks like he wants to beat me with my own head."

She giggled, leaning into him. "Wouldn't that be kinda hard?"

He cupped her cheek, conveniently hiding their mouths from Gabe. "Not if he rips it off first." His lips touched her ear. "He'd probably have it encased in resin and use it as a bowling ball so the pain would be eternal."

"I don't think you'd be feeling much pain in your bowling ball." She tapped his chin with her finger. "Now, if he decided to use your hollowed-out balls as castanets?"

He blinked and quickly hid his face against her shoulders. "I'm frightened. Hold me?"

She threw her head back and laughed, ignoring the anger beating at her skin like a living thing, desperate to break through the façade of cheer she held in front of her like a shield. She knew whose anger she was feeling, but she completely ignored her mate in favor of the human sitting next to her. Quite frankly, after months of ignoring Sarah, Gabe deserved to see what it felt like.

Jim's smile tickled the bite mark Gabe had left behind. "When did you get a hickey, Sarah?"

Her eyes went wide. "Um..."

"Did you burn yourself with curlers or something just to make him jealous?" He leaned back and put his arm around her shoulders, smiling at Gabe. "Gotta love a smart woman, eh, Gabriel?" he shouted across the table.

Gabe smiled back, showing more teeth than should be humanly possible. "Some women are smarter than others, I'll grant you that."

Her lashes lowered at the look on his face. She had the feeling that if they'd been in their dream her ass would be burning right now.

"Sarah? I need to speak to you privately."

She looked up at Gabe and noted the smile had turned into fierce determination. She opened her mouth to reply, not quite sure what she was going to say. Her heart was pounding, partly in fear, partially in anticipation.

Jim interrupted her before she could speak, kissing her cheek. "Are we still going dancing after dinner?"

She smiled sweetly up at Jim, taking the out he handed her, ruthlessly ignoring the seething man across the table from her. She knew at some point there would be a reckoning, but for now she was going to enjoy the support of her friend. Something about the way Gabe was watching her reminded her of what he'd been training to do for the last several months. "Sounds great!"

Jim picked up her hand and kissed her fingers again. A small shiver went through her, but not because of Jim. The two fingers Gabe tapped against his plate were a warning, and she knew it. Luckily the restaurant's animated animals chose that moment to begin their screams, distracting Jim from the golden-eyed glare Gabe was sending his way. That had to be giving him a headache. She'd never seen a Puma's eyes remain gold for so long.

Gabe's sudden turn-around was startling, and she didn't quite trust it. He'd spent the better part of two months ignoring her in favor of Chloe, but a couple of hours of Sarah flirting with Jim had him doing a countdown to a spanking? Hah!

The Pride leaders were standing, laughing and joking about dancing the night away over at Universal Studio's nightclubs. Her plan was to dance and have fun with the blond god next to her. She would deal with the consequences tomorrow. Tonight she had a date with a good friend and a little white pill that guaranteed her a dreamless sleep.

Gabe stood next to one of the many sofas that surrounded the dance floor and watched as his mate shimmied to the music with Jim. Part of him wanted to storm over and cart her off into the sunset.

The other part was stuck listening to Simon and Adrian while he sipped a beer and pretended to listen. At least she wasn't dirty dancing with the asshole.

Actually, he couldn't call what she was doing dancing. She looked like she was having spasms. He hid his grin behind his beer as he watched her happily gyrating to the music. The look on Jim's face as he watched his partner was priceless. He doubted the man would stay on the dance floor with her for much longer. He at least seemed to know what he was doing. Sarah, on the other hand…

"She looks like someone's poking her ass with a stick." Simon cocked his head, watching as Sarah's body bowed in a way that should have been physically impossible while standing. In fact, Gabe was surprised she *was* still standing.

Adrian shook his head sadly. "What I want to know is, does she thinks she's actually dancing?"

Simon cocked his head the other way, like he was studying some strange alien life-form and didn't quite know what to make of it. "That's dancing? I thought it was some sort of weird religious thing. I know I saw a few of those moves on the Discovery Channel."

"Yes, but were they done by humans?"

Gabe turned back to his two friends, not surprised to see them smirking at him. "Do I make fun of your mates?"

"Have any of them given you such a good reason to?" Adrian took a sip of his own beer, his gaze straying over to his pale fiancée. She sat on the sofa behind them, her sensitive eyes carefully shielded from the strobe lights by big white sunglasses. She was laughing and chatting with Becky and Belle. Rick hovered over the women, a small smile on his face as he listened to them chat, his massive arms crossed over his chest, hard, cold eyes softening as they rested on Belle.

"I don't think any of our mates would be, ah, brave enough to step out onto the dance floor like that," Simon laughed, his own gaze straying to Becky's wild head of curls. The big glass artist's face was full of happiness.

Gabe rolled his eyes, his attention drifting back to Sarah. Jim was laughing at something Sarah had said or done, but he kept his body at a distance, possibly fearing for his limbs. Gabe was okay with the way they were dancing together...for now. The moment a slow song came on, however, he was going to be on the dance floor. There was only so much he could stomach. Seeing Sarah in another man's arms was not an option. "I still need to mark her." And he had to do it before Jim got any closer to Sarah than he already was.

"You should have taken care of that before you left." Gabe shot Simon a look. The Beta slammed one large hand down on Gabe's shoulder. "What the hell were you waiting for?"

Gabe grimaced. "The Hunter who trained me told me it would make things a lot more difficult for both of us." He ran his fingers through his hair wearily. "I'm beginning to think taking his advice was a huge mistake."

Simon frowned. "Damn. Six months, knowing who your mate was but leaving her unclaimed? The dreams must have been driving you insane. I know they're what finally made me realize what my Puma had been telling me for months. I just wish I'd acted sooner, before she got hurt."

Gabe nodded. Simon would probably never forgive himself for not claiming Becky before Livia, the rogue Puma who had tried to make Emma and Becky's lives hell, had managed to hurt her. "Seeing the hickey I gave her in one of those dreams was surreal. It just solidified for me how big a mistake it was." It took him a moment to realize that the two men were staring at him, shock on their faces. "What?"

Adrian was the first to recover. "You bit her in a dream and the mark showed up for real?"

"Hickey. I gave her a hickey." What would have happened if he *had* marked her in the dream? Would they be going through this now?

"Whatever." Adrian frowned. "As far as I know, that's impossible."

Gabe shrugged. That jived with what Gabe knew, but nevertheless the mark was there. "Obviously not."

Simon kept watch on the women while Adrian and Gabe chatted, but Gabe could tell they had the Beta's full attention. The fact that the Alpha and Beta had been made, not born, meant that the two men occasionally ran across some aspect of being a shifter that was still new to them.

And wouldn't he have loved to be a fly on the wall when Jonathon Friedelinde, the old Alpha, had bitten the two men? He wondered how all of them had handled the inevitable arousal that would have spiked between them. He'd heard the sensation was incredibly intense. He figured their girlfriends must have walked funny for a week afterwards, but no way in hell would he say that out loud where Emma and Becky could hear it considering they'd been dating Livia and Belle at the time.

Come to think of it, perhaps he shouldn't mention it in front of Rick, either.

Adrian shrugged. "Well, as far as I know, the mate dreams are just that: dreams. What you do in them has no impact on your mate whatsoever."

"I know that's how it normally works, but she knew it was there. She even covered it with her hand." Gabe watched as Sarah attempted to twirl and nearly fell on a nearby couple. Jim's quick hands stopped her from a nasty fall. Gabe grumbled and wondered if he'd actually have to *thank* the asshole.

"Could it have something to do with the fact that she's the Omega?"

Gabe felt everything in him still. For the third time that night he was stunned. "Excuse me?" *Omega? She's the Omega? Since when?*

Then something else occurred to him. *But that means...* He turned, glaring at his mate as she danced with Jim. *That means she knows* exactly *how I feel about her being with Jim.* Omegas were the heart of the Pride. Just as the Marshal could feel the physical well-being each Pridemember, the Omega could sense their emotional state. Together they allowed the Alpha to zero in on individual problems within the Pride that he might otherwise overlook.

His grin was feral as he caught her eye and held up three fingers. *Oh, baby. That's three.* He wasn't surprised to see the hint of wariness on her face before she turned her attention back to her dance partner.

"Yeah. It's been informally confirmed. We all agreed to hold off on the formal announcement until after you got back from your training." Simon shrugged, looking vaguely uncomfortable.

"Really."

"Gabe." He turned back to Adrian, who was frowning at him. "You weren't here. From everything we saw and heard you were pursuing Chloe, not Sarah."

"What?" His jaw clenched. Sarah had leveled the same accusation at him. "What the hell are you talking about?"

Simon began ticking things off on his fingers. "The bracelet you gave Chloe for Christmas when you didn't bother giving Sarah a gift." Gabe flushed. He had a present for Sarah, he'd just wanted to give it to her in person. "You talk to Chloe almost every day, but don't call Sarah at all."

"Sarah stopped answering her phone." Gabe was becoming pissed. Even the Pride leaders thought he'd betrayed his mate with another woman?

Things were worse than he thought.

"And Chloe constantly talks about you and what you're doing, while Sarah knows next to nothing."

He frowned. That wasn't what he'd intended at all. Chloe was supposed to befriend Sarah, keep her company. When she'd stopped answering the phone he'd become worried about her. And from what Chloe had said Sarah was spending a lot of time with...

Aw hell. Please tell me that Chloe didn't deliberately sabotage my relationship with Sarah. "Christ, what a mess. I have to fix this."

Simon pointed with his chin towards the dance floor. "Go dance with your woman. Sounds like they're about to start a slow song." The big artist winked, grinning. "And with all those bodies dry-humping out there no one will even care if you give your mate a bite, will they?"

Gabe watched as the lights dimmed and Sarah stepped into Jim's arms. "I think you may be right."

It was past time to claim what was his.

Sarah knew the moment Gabe stepped up behind her. His heat and masculine scent enveloped her, despite the fact that she was in another man's arms. He reached around her and tapped Jim's shoulder. "May I cut in?"

Jim made a great show of reluctantly letting Sarah go, scowling at Gabe before giving her a light peck on the cheek and stalking away. She almost stopped him, terrified of what Gabe had planned for her. His emotions beat against her back, anger and remorse mixed with a primal need to stake his claim on her. His hands slipped around her waist, cradling him to her. His erection pressed against her lower back, the heat from his cock and the savage satisfaction that broke through at his touch making her weak in the knees. With him touching her there was no way she could completely shield herself from his emotions.

She searched frantically for a distraction, the thought of those three fingers he'd held up worrying her. She found it when Jim got stopped by Chloe. The two spoke for a moment and, with a shrug, he pulled her into his arms and onto the dance floor. The lust pouring off both of them was incandescent.

"Sarah." She shivered as he licked the mark on her neck, her attention suddenly riveted to the man behind her. His teeth scraped the sensitive juncture of her shoulder and she twitched. "Hold still, baby."

Oh, no you don't. Not that easily, and especially not in public. She pulled away, hunching her shoulders against his fangs. "No."

"No?" A feather-soft kiss caressed the nape of her neck. "Why no?"

She growled. "Gee, I don't know. Should we start with Chloe?"

"I told you I didn't sleep with her, Sarah." She turned in his arms, not surprised when he pulled her firmly against him. He patted her rear. "Or do I need to remind you of that conversation?"

She sniffed, her irritation growing when he smiled down at her lazily. "Fine. How about we talk about the fact that you've basically been ignoring me?"

"I called and you didn't answer. Or when you did, we fought." His jaw worked, the tension rolling off him almost nauseating her. "You couldn't come to me and I couldn't go to you, and it was driving us both insane."

"So you turned to another woman?"

He shook his head. "Chloe was supposed to make friends with you, to help you. Damn it, Sarah! I was worried bout you."

He had an odd way of showing it. "You're joking, right?"

"Chloe wasn't supposed to give you the impression we were dating. She was supposed to make sure you were all right. That's all. I promise you, the only thing I feel for Chloe is...God, she's like the sister I never had and now I'm glad I didn't get."

If it wasn't for the sincerity she could feel coursing through him, she'd cry bullshit. One of the things she'd discovered since becoming Omega was that it was damn difficult to lie to her. The guilt most people felt when lying tended to bleed through. Still, if he'd actually been that stupidly gullible she'd have to make sure he never, *ever* did something like that again. "If that was your plan, I have two words for you. Epic fail."

"I'll talk to Chloe. I promise you I will straighten this out."

She sneered. "Sure you will." And she would spend that time with Jim. At least he didn't leave her senses reeling.

"Sarah. You're my mate. *You.* Chloe is just a friend." His shoulders slumped, his head landing on her shoulder with a weary sigh. "I should have told James to fuck off and marked you before I left. You have no idea how sorry I am that I didn't."

Sarah rolled her eyes. She couldn't see *anyone* who wasn't Pride stopping Gabe from doing what he wanted to do unless he didn't want to do it.

He lifted his head. Whatever he saw on her face had one brow rising arrogantly. "Don't you think I regret not marking you before I left?"

"Not really, considering you've been free to get a fucking girlfriend."

His expression darkened. "That's five."

"Five?" She pushed back against his chest, straining against his hold. She just wanted to put a little space between them, but he wasn't allowing it.

"One for sitting next to Jim. Two for agreeing to go dancing with him. Three for doing it knowing *exactly* how I felt about it." His hand curved around the nape of her neck, holding her possessively. "Four for turning away from my mark. And now five for thinking I would *ever* betray you that way." The hand not caressing her neck smoothed down her back, landing to rest

164

just atop the curve of her ass. "Care to make it six?"

She scowled up at him. "Care to get your ass kicked?"

He threw his head back and laughed. "I thought so." His hand landed against her ass, smacking her right there on the dance floor. "Go ahead, baby. Keep pushing."

She glared at him but refused to answer. The flutter in her lower belly wouldn't let her. She was afraid if she opened her mouth she'd say something stupid like *Please fuck me.*

"Sarah."

She lowered her eyes. She couldn't help herself.

"Look at me, Sarah." She looked up at him to find that his expression was full of regret. "You stopped answering the phone. You stopped talking to me. So I asked Chloe to make friends with you so I'd know you were okay. I had no idea she'd give you the impression that the two of us were dating."

The pain of loss was still thrumming through her, and she wasn't certain she believed him about Chloe. It was the reason she'd turned to those little white pills Dr. Howard had given her. "Uh-huh. Sure. I called you back more than once, but you never returned *those* calls. Was that when you started turning to Chloe?"

"Chloe is only a friend." He growled when she snorted her disbelief. "Sarah." She shivered at his tone. She'd heard it in dreams, but never in reality. It demanded her attention, her obedience, and without thought she started to comply. He leaned down and blew on the side of her neck, right where the hickey was. She shivered in response, his smile tickling her skin. "You are my mate. The only woman I dream about is you." She could feel his arousal, the sensation heightening her own. She could also feel his determination and his possessiveness. Instead of smothering her, she felt cocooned by it, a warm blanket she could cuddle under for the rest of her life. He licked her neck. "Did you know that the dreams we share aren't normal?" He caressed her ass, moving her in time to the music, his fingers brushing the bottom curve of her ass. "Most people only dream of making love to their future mate." He lifted his head from her throat, catching her chin on the edge of his hand and turning her face up to his. "You and I actually make love."

"Why?" When he frowned down at her, she added, "Why did we wind up connected that way?"

"I don't know. Maybe it was because we didn't speak for so long, or maybe because you're the Omega."

That reminder was all she needed to pull back from him and the warm seduction he was tempting her with. "Or maybe it's because you didn't really want me."

"Damn it, Sarah." His long-suffering sigh was music to her ears.

"So you turned to Chloe."

His eyes narrowed, determination filling his features. "I'm not going to explain myself again. Listen carefully. You are my *mate*. The thought of touching anyone other than you is disgusting. Do you understand me?"

She lowered her lashes, hiding her gaze from his. He might think they were done with the topic, but she was far from done. "What happens when you leave again?"

He sighed and pulled her in close, cradling her head against his shoulder. "Don't worry, baby. Right now wild gorillas couldn't drag me away from you."

She sniffed, resisting the temptation to snuggle into his warmth. *Damn, he smells so good.* "What about wild waitresses?"

His chest rumbled as he growled. "That's seven."

He still wasn't sure why he'd allowed her to stop him from marking her right there on the dance floor, but he had to admit just the freedom to hold her in his arms was incredible. No more doubts, no worries, just him and his mate caressing each other with their bodies as the music seduced them. He buried his face in her hair, wallowing in her scent, imbedding it into his memory. He wanted to cover himself in that scent, to have her covered in his until he couldn't tell where one of them ended and the other began. And despite his words he knew he had a lot to make up for.

She tripped, almost pulling them to the floor. He caught her easily.

"Sorry." She buried her flaming cheeks against his chest again after granting him one glance full of embarrassment.

"I know how to keep you safe from falling."

She eyed him warily. "How?"

He smiled and lifted her so that her feet were dangling, enjoying her shocked gasp.

"Put me down, Gabe!"

"Look at me, Sarah." He used the same tone he used during their scenes, knowing what her instinctive response would be. He smiled gently when her head lifted, her face turning up to his. "Trust me." The uncertainty there tore at his heart, but it was his own fault, damn it. He'd do whatever it took to get her to believe in him again. "I will never let you fall."

"Don't you mean never again?"

"Hmm?" He rocked her gently to the music, her toes barely brushing the tops of his feet. He barely felt her weight. He frowned, studying her. Damn. She *was* thinner. Why hadn't he noticed before? He'd have to make sure to fix that, too. He couldn't let his baby get sick.

"You'll never let me fall again." She lowered her lashes, once again hiding her expression from him, but not before he saw the disbelief in her face and knew it wasn't a physical fall she referred to.

"Stop it." He set her down on her feet but kept her close. "I'm going to prove to you that you can trust me."

She stopped dancing. "I begged for you. I cried for you. And you turned away from me. Do you know how that feels?"

"No. Sarah–"

"It feels like *this!*"

Sharp, cutting pain, deep despair, rejection, jealousy, Gabe felt it all. Got savaged by what he'd done to his mate. He'd stayed away from her, tried to protect her from their separation. Instead, in refusing to claim her he'd nearly destroyed her. He damn near dropped to his knees, the agony ripping through him almost more than he could bear.

"Now all of a sudden you want to claim me? How can I trust that?"

The feelings, *her* feelings, shut off abruptly, but lingered in his heart, mingling with his own until he couldn't tell where his left off and hers began.

The tears in her eyes clawed at him. He wanted to lift his face and scream from the pain he'd inflicted on his sweet Sarah. "What do you want me to do, Sarah? Beg? Cry?" Because he'd do both just to get that look off her face, those emotions from her heart.

"No."

"Then what?"

Determination filled her face. "I want the same treatment you gave Chloe."

What? "What, exactly, do you mean by that?" Gabe was

starting to get seriously pissed off. The fact that Sarah *still* believed he'd somehow been with Chloe rankled. How could she continue to think he'd do that to her?

Easy, dickhead. Your friend went out of her way to make Sarah think it. He needed to sit Chloe down and find out what the hell had been going through her head. She *knew* how important Sarah was to him. Gabe almost growled in frustration but contained it. Sarah deserved her pound of flesh, but damn if he'd let her take too much or too long.

"I want to be *asked out*." Gabe blinked in surprise at her fierce tone. "I want dinner. I want dancing. I want to know that I'm the only one you want to be with. I want a fucking bracelet for Christmas." He winced. She didn't know it, but he'd gotten her something much better than a bracelet, but since she hadn't been home he'd held on to it. It wasn't the kind of gift he wanted her opening by herself. She blew out her breath, running her hands through her soft, shining hair. "I may submit to you in the bedroom, but I will be *damned* if you treat me like an unwanted toy outside of it." Her eyes narrowed. "When you've proven that to me, *then* I'll claim you."

He clenched his teeth and nodded. As punishments went this one wasn't all that bad.

"And no sleeping together, either. You'd probably mark me right in the middle and I'm not ready for that yet."

Okay, it was rapidly getting worse. "What *am* I allowed to do on these dates?"

"It's simple." She pulled out of his arms, her eyes weary and defeated, like she couldn't believe that he meant what he said. "Show me you love me."

He stared, stunned, as she turned and walked away from him. Finally he just shook his head. "Fuck." *Show* her he loved her? She was the goddamn Omega! Couldn't she *feel* it? His entire being ached for her!

He headed for Chloe, grabbing her arm and pulling her away from Jim Woods. "What the hell were you thinking?"

She blinked up at him, startled. "What?"

"When did we start dating, Chloe?"

Her mouth flew open. "Aw crap. Sarah too?"

Gabe looked over her shoulder to see Jim staring at them with a disgusted look. "Shit." He turned his gaze back down to Chloe. "I wonder where they got *that* idea."

"Don't you turn this back on me, Gabriel Anderson." She shook her finger in his face, looking for all the world like his grandmother. "You're the one who stopped calling your mate."

Fuck. She was right. "You're the one who *did* talk to her. What did you do, tell her I was calling you but forget to mention all we talked about was her and Jim?"

She grimaced. "She didn't give me many chances. I tried telling her how you were doing, what you were doing, but she started shutting me down."

Because it had looked like he was opening his life to Chloe but not to Sarah. "Damn it." He scrubbed his face. "And you were jealous of the time she spent with Jim."

Her face filled with guilt. "Maybe."

So whether they'd meant to or not they'd both screwed up their relationships with their mates. "We're so screwed."

"I'm sorry, Gabe." She put her hand on Gabe's arm in apology.

"I can make things up with Sarah, don't worry." He watched Jim stalk away, anger in every line of the other man's body. "But I'm not sure what we can do to fix you and Jim."

"Double crap." Chloe's shoulders slumped. "What do we do?"

He knew he looked like the predator he was when she shivered. "We claim our mates."

When the Pride leaders headed out the door of the club he followed, intent on one thing and one thing only.

Winning back Sarah's trust. Because whether she wanted to acknowledge it or not, he already knew he held her heart, just as she held his.

Chapter Five

She hadn't been able to stay in there one moment longer. She didn't know if anyone even noticed she'd gone. Gabe had gone straight to Chloe. *Surprise, surprise.* The other woman had immediately stopped dancing with Jim and gone off with Gabe, much to Jim's obvious disgust.

She stepped out of the club, breathing in the night air. She smiled at the milling people peppering Universal's City Walk, wondering where she could go to release some of the lingering tension from her confrontation with Gabe.

Ah, Rising Star. Just what I need. She pulled out her cell phone and texted Sheri and Belle, not wanting any of her Pridemates to worry about her.

The response surprised her. *Oh! Wait up!*

Within a few moments everyone was outside, including Chloe, damn it. She was talking to Gabe, her expression an odd mixture of chagrin and determination. Gabe's gaze latched on to Sarah, but she ignored it. So much for showing her who he wanted to be with. Sarah held back her frustrated scream through sheer willpower. She put a smile on her face and looked around for Jim, hoping he was willing to continue the game if Gabe stuck by Chloe.

"Ready?" Emma was grinning from ear to ear. Sarah wasn't so sure she was ready for the rest of the Pride to hear her sing.

"C'mon, Sare-bear, if you sing I'll sing." Belle put her arm around Sarah's shoulders, Jim taking up position on Sarah's other side. She ignored the quick surge of annoyance she felt from Gabe. He was beginning to earn his own strike-outs, damn it.

"Careful. Lean on Belle too much and you're all going down." Rick put his hand at his mate's back, wrapping it around her waist. Jim mimicked him at Sarah's waist. They stumbled awkwardly off the steps of the club, the two women sharing a giggle as the men tried gallantly to keep them on their feet. "Now, where are we going?"

Gabe reached around and literally plucked Sarah from Jim's side, making sure Belle was supported by her mate first. "Did someone mention Rising Star?" He set her down gently on her feet, wrapping his arm around her waist possessively, smiling smugly at Jim. Jim frowned but allowed himself to be distracted by Chloe, who grabbed his arm with a grin and began tugging him farther out onto the Walk.

Sarah decided not to struggle. The determination washing through her from him was fierce. She had the feeling that if she tried to get away he'd literally run her to ground. She was still a little pissed that he'd walked out with Chloe, though, so it was with great relish that she told him their plans. "Yup. I'm in the mood for karaoke."

Gabe stopped dead. So did every other male of the Pride, and the two male non-Pride members. "Karaoke? Rising Star is a karaoke bar?"

She blinked up at him innocently. "Yes."

He groaned. "I didn't know you were *that* mad at me."

Emma sailed past them with a wave. "Don't be a wuss, Gabe. After all, if Max can sing so can you."

Max lunged after Emma. "No way, Emma. I am not sticking

my ass up on stage and making a fool of myself."

The Curana pouted up at her mate. "Not even for me?"

"Emma."

Sarah kept walking, leaving her Alpha and his mate behind to argue it out, forcing Gabe to keep pace as she made her way to the bar. "I'm looking forward to this."

"I'm sure you are." Gabe was practically pouting.

She patted Gabe's arm. "Look on the bright side. I'm not trying to force you to sing."

"No?" Gabe held open the door for her and let her inside, following swiftly on her heels. His eyes scanned the area even as his body moved between her and the crowd, protecting her from any would-be threats. His Hunter training was peeking out of his civilized veneer. It shouldn't turn her on, but it did. She had the stupidest urge to pet his muscles.

"No." She followed him to a back booth large enough to hold their party. *"I'm* going to sing."

Gabe seated her then followed her in, placing himself at the edge of the booth. One brow rose in disbelief. "You are?" The others quickly took seats, Chloe somehow managing to finagle a seat next to Jim.

"Mm-hmm."

"She's got a great voice." Belle winked at Sarah, her smile huge. "She's going to knock your socks off."

Sarah poked Gabe in the side hoping to get him to move. "Speaking of which, let me go sign up for my turn. Belle, you in?"

"Sure!"

Belle was practically bouncing, much to Rick's obvious amazement. "Oh, this I have *got* to see."

Belle put her hands on her waist. "Hey, I can sing!"

"Sweetheart, I was there for the infamous mojito night. Trust me, what you do in no way resembles singing."

Everyone laughed as Belle glared at Rick. "I am *so* going to enjoy proving you wrong, Fido."

The big man just shook his head and smiled, the love he held for his Luna written all over his face. Sarah sighed, wondering if she'd ever see a look like that on Gabe's face. "I'm going to enjoy watching you *try*."

"Five bucks says I get up there and leave you begging for more." Belle's chin lifted, her haughty stare challenging Rick.

Rick's answer was a simple lift of one brow and a five-dollar bill slapped on the tabletop. Two seconds later Belle's five was plunked down on top of it.

"Sucker," Sarah snickered. The Wolf didn't know it but that five was as good as lost.

"Why do I have the feeling you know something Rick doesn't?"

Gabe's whisper in her ear sent shivers down her spine. Ruthlessly she squashed them. She was nowhere near ready to forgive him yet. "You'll see."

Fingers tangled gently in her hair, a slight tug at the nape of her neck reminding her of who she was dealing with. "I guess I will," was all he said, but his hand gave one more tug before landing on her shoulder. His fingers caressed the mark he'd left on her neck.

She could feel him studying her, watching the emotions that crossed her face. She lowered her lashes, not wanting him to see into her soul. That was a right he needed to earn.

Gabe stood, holding back a frustrated sigh, and held out his hand. "Let's get you and Belle signed up for your songs." He held out his other hand for Belle, helping her from her seat. "I'll bring your mate right back, Rick."

Rick shook his head at Belle and fingered one of the five-dollar bills still sitting on the table.

Sarah was smiling, but it looked forced. Maybe he'd pushed a bit, tugging on her hair that way, but he couldn't seem to get her to focus on him, and he needed her to concentrate on him more than he needed to breathe. The only thing he could think of to do was be himself and just hope she would let him make everything up to her. He took Sarah's hand, wanting the feel of her near him, hiding a wince when she tried to pull her fingers away. A little telltale glance at Chloe told him what the problem was. Apparently he had a *lot* of making up to do. Her reaction to his walking out of the club with Chloe hadn't even occurred to him until he'd seen the look on her face. Maybe if she knew what they'd been talking about it would help ease the sting of his own stupidity.

He was so damn tired of seeing that bleak, hurt expression. He'd pulled away from Chloe the moment he saw it but by then she'd turned away. Turned to Jim. The fucker. He took a deep breath and reminded himself that Sarah wouldn't appreciate Jim's blood on her pretty dress.

"Anyone else?" Sarah's voice dragged him away from his thoughts.

"Sorry, I couldn't carry a tune if you put it in a bucket and painted the handle with crazy glue." Everyone stared at Sheri. "What?"

Sarah shrugged. "Okay, anyone else?"

Surprisingly, Rick stood. He stared down at his openmouthed mate. "What are we waiting for?" He took her arm and led her over to the sign-in sheet.

Gabe shook his head and followed, Sarah's hand clasped in

his. He didn't miss the wink Jim sent her, either. *The little minx. That's eight.* He began cataloging ways to hide the vet's body. It was all he could do not to snarl at the other man. "Do you know what song you want to sing?"

She flipped through the selection, studying each one carefully. Belle had already made her selection, as had Rick. "That one."

Her selection shouldn't have surprised him but it did. He grinned as she wrote her name and selection down and handed them to the DJ. "Sunshine Superman?"

"Mm-hmm."

He led her back to the booth to wait for her turn to sing, hoping he'd be able to get her to relax and let him in, even a little bit. His first step was pulling her into his arms as soon as they were seated, refusing to allow her to move. The flush that stole over her cheeks was worth the amused, knowing looks his Pridemates sent their way. *Now to set the record straight.* "Chloe and I were talking about her mate."

He felt her muscles jump under his hands. "Her mate?"

He nodded, his lips set against her neck. "Mm-hmm. She knows who he is but he doesn't seem interested." The music started back up. Unless he wanted to scream in her ear, he'd have to wait to give her any more information.

Having Sarah in his arms made everything worth it. He nuzzled her hair, ignoring the screeching of the half-drunk man on stage. He allowed the quiet peace of having his mate's scent and warmth beside him to lull him, feeling serene for the first time in months.

I'm going to throw up. Sarah rubbed at her stomach and swallowed hard. She stared out into the audience as the first strains of her song started up, the knowledge that Gabe was

177

there making everything ten times worse. *Why, oh why, did I decide to do this? And how did I wind up singing before both Belle and Rick? They signed up before me!* She took a deep breath, almost ready to bolt.

A pair of midnight blue eyes stared up at her from the edge of the stage. Gabe smiled, laughter lighting up his face. She could feel the rueful amusement coming off him and knew he expected her to suck almost as bad as the last person who had been up on the stage. The woman had missed every single note of her song, but she'd had so much fun that Sarah had clapped almost as loud as the girl's boyfriend.

Sarah glared at Gabe, determined to prove him wrong. Her stomach settled down and the music began. She saw her cue, the joy of the song pushing everything else from her mind. Sarah belted out the lyrics, staring into Gabe's incredibly handsome face, seeing the astonishment and, yes, pride growing there. What made it even better was the envy she could see on Chloe's face as the woman stopped next to him.

Hah! Take that, man-stealing bitch! Now that she'd started, Sarah was having a blast. The lyrics matched her mood perfectly. Sheer possessiveness put an extra swing into her hips as she sang. "'Cause I've made my mind up, you're going to be mine." She made sure she was leaning over for that part, challenging Gabe before turning away from him to sing to the rest of the audience. When the instrumental part started she danced before picking up with the lyrics once more. "When you've made your mind up forever to be mine, I'll pick up your hand and slowly blow your little mind." She turned, shimmying her ass right in Gabe's face, ignoring the hands he held up. Nine fingers. *Oh, shit. My ass is going to be sore.* She threw her head back and laughed, finishing the song with a flourish before accepting his hand off the stage.

The soft tap to her ass made her jump, a reminder of what

lay ahead. "Little mind?"

The affectionate teasing threading through his voice reassured her enough to have her tease him back. "All things considered, I'd dare to call it tiny."

"Ouch." He patted her rear. "Fine, score one for you."

"Yes!" She marked a point on an imaginary scoreboard with her finger. Gabe's love tap on her ass was a little sharper, but he rubbed the sting away almost immediately. Sarah was left blinking, fighting her sudden arousal when they reached the table.

Emma was clapping. "Way to go, Sarah!"

"Not bad, Sare-bear!" Sheri gave her two thumbs-up. Adrian merely smiled and nodded, his attention almost immediately returning to Sheri.

Simon and Becky both looked like they'd taken a drink of water and gotten a mouthful of good wine instead, but both high-fived her. Max, for some obscure reason, looked and felt smug, like he'd known all along that she could do it.

Gabe helped her into her seat and settled her between his legs, the bench allowing him to cradle her between his thighs. She allowed it, the feel of his arms wrapping around her waist and the praise of her friends drugging her senses with sweet warmth. Almost as wonderful was the feeling of contentment she could feel pouring off Gabe, like everything he'd ever needed was right there in front of him. Hell, he was even *purring*. She looked over at Chloe to find the other woman watching them with a wistful expression and a sad smile. Sarah turned away, unwilling to analyze why she felt guilty about Gabe cuddling her in front of the other woman.

She almost missed Belle limping onto the stage, smiling sweetly as the opening strains of Jewel's "Hands" started up, startling them. Belle looked like an angel sitting in the light of the stage, her hair a golden halo around her head. She lifted the mic and Sarah sat back, prepared to watch the others get impressed.

Gasps sounded around the table as Belle's strong, gentle voice floated over them. "Holy shit. She's good." Gabe shook his head. "Why didn't we know that?"

Sarah tilted her head back, the top of her head brushing Gabe's cheek. "Bimbo persona, remember? Besides, Livia would have had a fit if she'd known Belle was good at something she wasn't, so Belle hid it." Stupid, but there it was. Belle had given Livia a loyalty the rogue hadn't been worthy of and had wound up paying a price she hadn't deserved.

"Well she's certainly not hiding it now." She would have bristled over the admiration in Gabe's voice if it wasn't for the fact that she could *feel* it. It had nothing to do with lust and everything to do with friendship.

The pride he'd felt when Sarah had sung had been mixed with a healthy dose of lust and…love? Sarah shook her head, not certain she'd felt what she thought she had. How could it be love? She just couldn't trust her senses where Gabe was concerned. It was entirely possible she was reading something into his emotions that just weren't there. Wishful thinking could wind up with her heart breaking all over again, and it had barely begun to mend.

Belle's face tilted up, her eyes closing as she sang. Rick stood at the edge of the stage, a strange look on his face, utter disbelief mingled with astonished pride, *his* love singing across her senses. "Apparently Rick didn't know either."

"I guess." Gabe picked up a drink and handed it to her. "Strawberry margarita."

"When did you get this?"

"Just before your song started up. I thought you might be

thirsty afterwards."

"Thank you." She took a sip just as Belle's song ended to thunderous applause. When Belle went to get off the stage Rick stopped her, settling her back down on the stool. "Oh, this should be good."

"Have you heard him sing?" Gabe began peppering kisses around the hickey he'd given her.

"Hmm?" The feel of Gabe's mouth on her skin nearly turned off her brain. *Rick, right.* "Nope, but I bet he's better than we expect."

"Why?"

"He seems like the type of guy who wouldn't put himself out there like that unless he was pretty sure he could rock it."

"True."

They turned to watch the big redhead take the mike. He nodded to the DJ, holding Belle's hand in his. Eric Clapton's "Change the World" started to play. Belle smiled up at her mate as he crooned to her.

Sarah could feel the mood of the room as Rick sang, the women swaying into their dates as the big bad Wolf showed the world exactly how he felt about his Belle. The feelings swept over her, mellow and sweet, and Sarah swayed with them, lapping them up like a chocoholic in a Hershey's factory.

Gabe's hand began stroking her stomach in tender circles. He began to croon into her ear along with the song, distracting her from the emotions floating around her. Sarah licked her lips. Gabe's voice was nowhere near as smooth as Rick's, but it affected her much more deeply. She lowered her eyes and leaned back against Gabe, feeling his jolt of surprised joy when she did so, soaking in the sense of safety only being in his arms gave her. It was like the dreams, but so much better, knowing he was actually there behind her. She let her worries and fears

181

drift away on the song in her ears and her heart.

Gabe tilted up her face with a firm hand, placing a soft kiss on her lips before cuddling her close. That first real taste of her mate left her senses reeling, but the sight of Chloe across from them brought her sharply to her senses. She straightened, pulling away from him, much to his annoyance. She could feel it, sharp and tingly. She couldn't give in, not yet. Not until the question of Chloe was answered to her satisfaction.

Rick's song ended to thunderous applause. Bowing, he led Belle off the stage and right out the door of the club, the blonde's happy laughter trailing behind them, the two five-dollar bills still sitting on the table, forgotten by them both.

"Now I wonder where he's taking her." Gabe's shoulders shook as he laughed.

Sarah shook her head. You didn't need to be Omega to figure that one out.

Chapter Six

Gabe held onto Sarah's hand and his own hopes for the evening. He knew how he wanted the evening to end, but from the hot-and-cold way Sarah was blowing he had no clue whether or not he'd get his wish. He wanted to drag her into his room, tie her down and deliver each and every one of those spankings he'd promised her. He wanted to watch her beg for his cock while he tongued her luscious pussy. He wanted to come so deep inside her she'd be marked before he ever bit down on her sweet neck. He wanted to hear her purr as he rocked her to sleep.

If he had his way she'd never get a chance to say no.

When they reached the staircase, she paused. One way led to Gabe's room; the other, to Sarah's. From the hesitation on her face he had the feeling his dream of having her in his arms tonight wasn't going to be a reality.

His dream... That was the key, wasn't it? He might not have known it at the time but they'd been controlling their mate dreams ever since they first started. Gabe smiled, knowing full well how predatory it looked. He had every intention of controlling their dream tonight.

Tonight he would show her he loved her.

He turned left, ignoring her small sigh of relief. He walked her to her room, the perfect gentleman, ready and willing to leave her at her door for just one small favor in return. "Sarah." She turned and looked up at him, a question on her face. "Let me in tonight."

She grimaced. "Gabe—"

He put his finger to her lips, gratified at her immediate silence. "I'm leaving you at your door, unmarked, giving you a little time to learn to trust me again." He leaned in, nipping at her ear, smiling as her breath stuttered. "But in return, I want you to *let me in.*" He cupped her cheek and turned her face up to his. "I want sweet dreams for both of us tonight. Whatever you've been doing to turn off the mate dreams, *please* don't do it tonight. Understood?"

She licked her lips, the uncertainty back on her face. "I'm not sure I can."

He growled, displeased.

She was shaking her head. "How am I supposed to...do that with you when I don't know if I can trust you?"

He took a deep breath, trying to bury the rage that threatened to overwhelm him. If she sensed it at all she'd be afraid that he was enraged with *her.* The fact was he couldn't believe his own stupidity. She was right. A true relationship required trust on the part of both partners, a trust he'd lost by listening to the wrong person for the right reasons. "What will it take to make you believe you're the only woman I want?"

"More than one night of playing my boyfriend!"

"Playing?" He backed her up against her door, ignoring the alarm on her face. "You think I'm *playing?*" He took her by her shoulders, lifting her onto her toes. "Don't lie to me! You know *exactly* how I feel." He dropped her abruptly as a sudden thought struck him. "But this isn't really about trust, is it?" He took a step back. "It's about punishing me because I left before I marked you." Her mouth was hanging open in shock. He sighed and ran his fingers through his hair, all of his anger draining, suddenly weary beyond belief. "Dream with me tonight." He swallowed, suddenly terrified that she wouldn't be able to give him even that much. "Please."

She studied him, slowly relaxing. He was grateful for whatever it was she saw when she whispered, "All right."

He closed his eyes in thanks before nodding. He wanted desperately to kiss her good night but didn't know if it would be welcome. What he wouldn't give to have Sarah's ability to read emotions. "Good night, love."

She started, frowning up at him, obviously confused. "Um. Good night, Gabe."

He turned reluctantly away, not trusting himself to keep his hands off her.

"Gabe?"

He looked back.

She looked so alone, almost as alone as he felt. "Spend the day with me tomorrow?"

He smiled. "There is *nothing* I want more." When she cocked her brows in disbelief he chuckled. "All right, there are one or two things I'd like more, but I'll take what I can get."

She nodded, opening her door. She stopped, hesitating before entering. "See you in a little bit."

She rushed into the room, the door clanging shut behind her, missing the step he'd taken in her direction before he could stop himself.

God, it was hard to walk away from her. He headed straight to his room, mulling over what he would do once they were together in their dreams. This had to work. She had to trust him again, because if she didn't he was going to mark her and deal with the consequences after.

Sarah leaned against the closed door of her room, her breath leaving her lungs in a rush. She'd just agreed to meet Gabe in their dreams, with no promise from him that it wouldn't turn into yet another night of debauchery.

She pushed off the door, running her hands over her face, trying to decide whether or not she'd done the right thing by sending him on his way. *What is* wrong *with me? One minute I want to open up the door, yank him back in and forget all about our problems. The next I want one of those pills and about three thousand miles of distance!* Maybe if she allowed him to mark her some of that fear would evaporate. But months of rejection weren't about to be erased in one evening.

She brushed her teeth and hair, draped the red dress over a chair and crawled into bed naked. It felt oddly wicked, since she usually slept in a nightgown, but tonight she wanted the feel of cool sheets on her skin. She could pretend that he was actually in the next room, waiting to crawl into bed with her after a long day's work. Sarah yawned, curling up on her side, and waited for sleep (*and Gabe,* her inner kitty purred) to claim her.

Sarah stared around the strange living room, her heart pounding as she realized where she must be. Gabe's scent was everywhere, deeply ingrained into the very wood of the house. If he didn't live here she'd be very surprised.

What she was completely surprised by was the look of his home. From the exterior it was a typical cookie-cutter ranch-style home, with a small front porch, beige aluminum siding and forest green doors and shutters. But on the inside it was a riot of rich colors mingled with deep earth tones. The hardwood floors looked like rough oak but were smooth under her bare feet. A bold geometric rug in yellow, green, red and dark brown was soft under her feet. The dark red was picked up in the contemporary sofa. Pale green and yellow throw pillows were tossed haphazardly at one end, a velvety blanket thrown over its back, the deep yellow color vibrant against the red fabric of the sofa. Mission-style stained glass and iron lamps sat on oak end tables. The walls were a soft shade of green, with thick oak baseboards and crown molding. A flat-screen TV sat on a wooden stand, a Playstation and Wii both hooked up to it. She smiled at the sight of the bright blue stoneware mug on the coffee table, the scent of its cooling contents letting her know that Gabe liked his sugar and cream with a little bit of coffee.

For all its bright color the room seemed to her to be missing something elemental, something that would make it truly a home. She picked her way across the room, wondering what that something was. She headed to the small kitchen, again done in the same bold colors.

No Gabe. She left the kitchen, turning down a hallway. The first door she came to was a small bedroom turned into a home office. She smirked at the sight of the papers scattered across its surface. The next room held a bathroom, this one in muted blues and greens. The next room was a small bedroom containing a single bed and a small dresser.

Last room. He's got to be in there. Sarah opened the door...

...and stepped into a quiet summer evening. A breeze ruffled her hair, bringing with it the faint tang of the ocean. Her bare feet slipped into cool sand, the grains tickling between her toes. She smiled, burying her toes in and wiggling them just to feel that sensation. She'd always loved doing that as a child.

"Hey."

She turned to find Gabe standing there in nothing but dark shorts and a T-shirt. In his hands was a huge picnic basket. "Hey."

"You look beautiful."

She blinked and looked down. She was wearing the same red sundress she'd worn for dinner that night. "Thank you."

He gestured with his hand towards the beach. "After you."

She smiled and began to walk. "Since when is your house on the beach?"

He shrugged. *"This is a dream."*

They walked until, somehow, the spot seemed just right. Sarah waited until Gabe had laid down the blanket, anchoring it with the basket and both of his sandals. "Sit, Sarah."

She sat, folding her legs beneath her.

"Good girl."

She looked up at him. "I thought we weren't playing any games tonight."

She watched him sit in front of her, his own legs crossed. He dug into the basket without answering.

"Gabe?"

The heated look he shot her sent shivers down her spine. Her nipples tightened in response to the predatory gleam in his eyes. "Who says I'm playing?"

She opened her mouth to answer, startled when he popped something in her mouth. She bit down without even thinking twice. Mmm. Chocolate-covered strawberries. She moaned around the succulent fruit, her eyes closing in bliss. As far as Sarah was concerned there was no better sweet treat to be had.

Wait a moment.

The beach, the moonlight, chocolate-covered strawberries... Uh-oh. She resisted the urge to roll her eyes. Talk about cheesy seduction tropes. Any second now he's going to break out champagne or something and I'm going to lose it and earn another spanking. This was so not Gabe. He was wild and bold and took what he wanted. It was one of the things she loved about him.

What was he thinking?

She opened her eyes to find Gabe studying her closely.

Testing out a theory, she pictured a big steaming bowl of spinach in the basket in place of the strawberries.

"Like the strawberries, love?" He reached behind him and produced a bottle of champagne and one crystal flute.

Here we go. She did her best to look as innocent as possible. "Yes, thank you."

His smile was slow. "Good." He put his hand into the basket, the smile quickly transforming into something like horror. "What the...?" He pulled his fingers, now covered in warm spinach, out of the basket. "What the hell?"

Sarah giggled.

He pulled a napkin out of the basket, his expression filled with amused disgust. "Why did you turn my strawberries into spinach?"

Sarah zipped her lips and waited for him to open the "champagne".

His eyes narrowed. He pulled out a corkscrew and began opening the bottle. He lifted the cork to his nose with a suspicious glare. "Ginger ale." He sighed, his lips lifting into a rueful grin. "I suppose I shouldn't even bother with the violin music. See what happens when I try to do this right?"

"Do what right?"

"Seduce you."

"Ix-nay on the beach sex." She shuddered. "Sand in very

uncomfortable places, plus, hello! Chafing much?"

His eyes turned gold. "How do you know that?"

Sarah smirked. "I'm sorry, Gabe. Were you a virgin when you came back to Halle?"

His cheeks flushed, the gold in his eyes dying down to sparkles. "Point taken, and we'll never mention it again." He lifted the bottle. "You told me that you wanted me to take you on dates, show you what you mean to me."

Sarah nodded. "I did."

"So what did I do wrong?"

"This, it just isn't you." She waved her hand at their surroundings. "It's beautiful, and wonderful, but..." She sighed. "I want the real Gabe to show me what I mean to him."

One dark brow rose, his lips curving in a wicked smile that had her nipples hard in seconds. "Be careful what you wish for, baby."

She gasped as the ground shifted beneath her. Suddenly she was on her knees in the middle of a wide bed, her arms cuffed over her head. A chain connected to those cuffs rose to a wood beam high in the white ceiling. She still wore the red dress, but the straps were no longer on her shoulders. Instead, it pooled at her hips, exposing her bared breasts to Gabe's intense gaze.

"Much better," he purred, picking up a leather-lined paddle. "I believe I owe you how many?"

Sarah's pussy quivered at the question. Oh fuck. I should have stuck to champagne. But she could no more resist answering than she could stop the arousal quivering through her body. But nothing says I can't play too. Besides, she had told him no sex. She lowered her head before he could see the grin threatening to overtake her face. "Three, sir."

"Good girl."

She shivered as his palm caressed her cheek. "Trust me, love."

Splat!

The expression on Gabe's face was worth the slimy feel of the pasta. "Sarah."

She bit her lip before responding. The cautious way he said her name told her he was fighting his own laughter. Thank God. She'd been afraid he would become angry. "Yes, sir?"

"Cooked spaghetti, Sarah? You had me whip you with wet noodles?"

She lost it, laughing so hard the chains rattled.

A hard hand grasped her chin. "Who's playing games now?" He shook his head at her and chuckled. "You win, love." The room disappeared and suddenly it was just the two of them on Gabe's red sofa. He had his arm wrapped around her shoulders, his hand holding hers in his lap. Their bare feet were up on his coffee table, the mug of coffee gone. "No more games." He brushed his cheek against her hair and purred.

She sighed and leaned against him, breathing in his scent, scarcely daring to believe he was cuddling with her. All of their other dreams had been sensual buffets. This was nice. "What do you want to do tomorrow?"

He toyed with her fingers. "We don't have anything wedding-related tomorrow. I'd like to walk around Disney, just the two of us."

He sounded so wistful. How could she resist? "Epcot? Magic Kingdom?"

He smiled. From the vibe coming off him he already had an idea or two. "We'll see."

"I wanted to go shopping in the World Showcase." Gabe

grimaced and she laughed. "I'll have to see if I can bribe you, then."

Quiet.

"Notice I'm being very good and not mentioning what my favorite bribe is."

Sarah buried her face in his shoulder. She knew exactly what his favorite bribe was, but she was sticking fast to her no-sex rule, at least for now. "I think you just did."

"Damn. I'll just have to come up with something else then."

She lifted her head and smiled up at him, unable to hide the warmth she felt. It was just so right to be sitting there holding hands and making plans. The fact that little purring noises kept slipping from him while he nuzzled her hair had her damn near ready to break her rule. It was like he and his Puma were wallowing in her scent. "I'm sure you will."

His eyes glittered with gold. "So am I." He captured her lips in a quick, hard kiss. "Now I think it's time we both rested before I'm tempted to try something again. I'll pick you up for breakfast around eight thirty."

"All right." She stood and headed for the front door, knowing it was the right thing to do in order to leave their dream peacefully. He stood and followed, opening the door onto his front lawn. "Good night, Gabe."

He pulled her close, leaning in for a good-night kiss that started sweet but ended with her bent to his will, his mouth devouring hers, tempting her to stay. The reluctance she felt when he pulled away from her spoke volumes. "Good night, love."

He closed the door before she could find out if he really meant to call her that.

She turned and strolled down the walkway, fingering her

lips and wondering if, just if, he really did.

    If only she could trust the dream.

Chapter Seven

He watched her bounce down the stairs of the Coronado Springs resort, her hair swinging, her full lips smiling, and her face filled with the joy of a new day. Dark sunglasses hid her eyes from him, but the brown shorts and dark blue tank top did little to hide her curves.

Hopefully she now knew how much he loved her.

He'd put everything he was into that last dream kiss, bending her, dominating her, leaving her breathless and panting and leaning against him weakly. And then he'd shut the door and let her walk away, fighting his instincts and his Puma the entire fucking time until he'd slipped out of their dream and into real, dreamless sleep. The blue balls that followed had not been his idea of fun, but he refused to take care of the problem without Sarah. The anticipation would make finally taking her all the sweeter, and today he had every intention of doing just that.

Today was going to be fun. The Pride was hitting the parks, enjoying being in Disney World before the wedding madness truly began. Tomorrow there were other activities planned, but today was all about being little kids again. Except the games Gabe wanted to play weren't at all child-like.

He couldn't wait to see Sarah's reactions. He stood, smiling at her as she came to a stop at the shuttle stop in the parking lot of the hotel. "Ready?"

She frowned, looking around. "Where's everyone else?"

"Magic Kingdom." And hadn't they laughed their asses off at him as he'd waved them on. They knew exactly what he was up to and approved of his plans. Hell, Emma had even added a suggestion of her own, something he knew Sarah would love to do with him. And she'd *definitely* approved of shopping the World Showcase, to no one's surprise.

He took Sarah's hand and led her to where the shuttle stop was. "I thought we might want to do Epcot. Ride Mission Mars, see Soaring, maybe go shopping in World Showcase."

She looked up at him with suspicion. "Shopping."

He did his best to look innocent. "Yes. Shopping."

"You seemed less than enthusiastic last night."

"Hey, I can shop. You hunt down your purchase, club it to death with a credit card and drag it out of the store, right?"

She sputtered.

"See? Men can shop just fine." He puffed up his chest, hoping to get her to laugh. "And I have special training as a Hunter, so I should be extra good at it."

She was trying her damndest to hide her grin, but it wasn't working. "Did Emma put you up to this?"

"I plead the fifth."

"Aren't we supposed to meet the others for dinner?"

"That *might* have been the plan at some point."

"Gabe."

He watched, smug satisfaction on his face as one of the shuttles pulled up, her hand curled firmly in his. "Sarah. Will you go out with me today?"

She bit her lip to keep from laughing as he helped her onto

the shuttle marked Epcot. "Gee, I don't know. Maybe I should think about it."

He sat next to her, his arm going around the back of the bench. "You do that."

She giggled. "Didn't we already agree to spend the day together?"

"Mm-hmm."

She eyed him sideways, a spark of mischief in her eyes. "So, where's your date?"

He growled. "How sore do you want your ass to be?" He put on his most dominant face, the one that never failed to make her lashes lower and her breathing speed up. "Don't make me tell you again, Sarah. *Nothing. Happened.*"

After a brief hesitation her lashes lowered, her head tilting down in submission. *Good.* Maybe he'd overreacted, but he was damn sick and tired of hearing her call Chloe his girlfriend. "Yes, sir."

Her quiet whisper was music to his ears. "C'mere." He pulled her close to him, as close as the molded plastic seats would let him, and watched the streets roll by, content just to breathe her in.

Sarah stifled a laugh as Gabe settled warily into the "cockpit" of Mission Space. "C'mon, Gabe, it's not *that* bad."

He shot her a lethal look as he pulled down the harness. "You had to pick the Orange team, didn't you?" The Orange version of the ride was a lot more energetic than the Green version.

She coughed into her hand. "Wuss." He opened his mouth to reply when the whine of the ride started. "Navigator. Cool.

Don't forget to stop and ask for directions."

He grumbled as the woman seated next to her laughed. "Yours too? My husband never stops for directions."

Sarah turned to answer just as the shuttle "lifted", the G-force pushing her back in her seat. After that, she was too busy punching buttons and laughing like a loon to answer anything. Even better were Gabe's muttered curses as the ride shook and shimmied, dived and soared.

"We are heading to Hollywood Studios and riding Tower of Terror." Gabe helped her out of the shuttle when the ride ended, a fierce grin on his face.

"Is that the dropping elevator ride?"

"Yup." He pulled her through the store and out the door, looking like an eager kid.

Sarah, however, was not so eager. "Nuh-uh. No way."

"Yes, way."

"Try no way in hell, then."

He laughed. "I got on Mission Space for you. You can get on Tower of Terror for me."

She thought quickly. She was *not* doing a falling-anything ride. "I thought we were going to go shopping in World Showcase and have an early dinner. Maybe we could watch the fireworks?" She gave him her best hopeful grin.

He didn't buy it. "I tell you what. I'll make you a deal. We head over to World Showcase now, have an early dinner, do a little shopping and then head to Hollywood Studios. If the Tower of Terror has more than a twenty minute wait, you're off the hook. But, twenty minutes or less, and we ride. Deal?"

She looked around. This time of year there weren't as many guests in the park. They hadn't gone for a ride other than Mission Space that had a longer than twenty-minute wait.

197

Then again, the Test Track and Spaceship Earth had had a very long wait and they hadn't even bothered. Maybe Tower of Terror would be swamped, too. It was supposed to be pretty popular. "Deal."

They started walking, the warm, humid air coating them both in a fine sheen of sweat before they'd gone very far. Gabe took hold of her hand, the absent gesture saying more than words could. "So, where would you like to eat?"

They walked over the bridge to World Showcase, landing in Mexico, and Sarah had a sudden yen for Mexican. "Oh. Can we?"

He picked up her hand and kissed it. "Sure."

They headed into the San Angel Inn, loving the Mexican market set up outside the restaurant. Sarah browsed the serapes and maracas while Gabe got their pager.

"About a half-an-hour wait until they can seat us. I thought we might shop."

"And you said it without shuddering, too!" She patted his head, laughing when he rolled his eyes.

He picked up her hand and took her into one of the shops, smiling indulgently as she oohed and aahed over the turquoise and opal jewelry. Then he took her on the indoor boat ride, holding her hand as they chased a video Donald through Mexico.

It was all so *normal* Sarah had a hard time believing it wasn't another dream.

When the pager went off Sarah was starving. They settled in, sharing a delicious meal of sangria and grilled fish. *Yum.* Pleasantly buzzed from dinner they made their way back into the World Showcase.

"Where would you like to shop first?"

She grinned up at Gabe, wondering if this too was a dream. "Italy. I want some Murano glass."

"Italy it is."

"And I want to stop in Japan and look at the Mikimoto pearls."

His smile was beginning to look strained. It was quite a hike from Mexico to Japan. "Okay."

"Oh! And I want to hit Morocco."

"With what?"

She laughed, swinging their hands as she practically skipped along the sidewalk, too happy to care about the differences between dreams and harsh realities.

Sarah grimaced as she stared at the sign next to the entrance of the Tower of Terror. "Fifteen-minute wait."

He gave her a ferocious grin, knowing he was as good as on the ride. "We had a deal."

"I know."

She sounded so disgusted he nearly laughed out loud. He practically dragged her into line, ignoring her muttering and dire threats of bodily injury. He was going to ride the Tower of Terror, and his mate was going to ride it with him. She'd given her word and she was going to stick to it.

They got into line. There were so few people waiting it took only a moment for them to walk through the doors. Following the cattle run, Gabe tried to calm Sarah's anxiety. "It's not that bad."

"Have you ever been on it before?"

"Once."

He wondered what his face looked like, because she paled

and gulped. He'd *loved* the ride. If he hadn't had to leave to meet some friends he would have gone on it more than once. "You're gong to *like* this."

"Or else?"

He snorted. "Worrywart."

They stepped onto the elevator and took their seats. "Gabe?"

He heard a tremor in her voice and suddenly wondered if he'd done the right thing. Her hand was trembling in his. He hadn't meant for her to be *this* scared. "Want to get off?" He'd ride by himself. No, he'd get off with her. He wasn't letting her out of his sight.

She sat. She was biting her lip, but she strapped herself in, staring forward like she'd just strapped herself down in an electric chair.

That's my girl. "Hold my hand. Trust me, it's really not that bad."

Five minutes later, as they hung suspended before they dropped yet again, she turned to him and calmly stated, "I hate you."

Her screams pierced his ears as he laughed and laughed.

When they stumbled off the ride and back into the sunshine he was still laughing. "Aw, c'mon, it wasn't *that* bad." He tugged on her hand, stopping her as she tried to stomp away from him.

"Neither was being a freshman in high school but I wouldn't want to repeat it."

He pulled, hard, ignoring her squawk of protest when she landed in his arms. He kissed the tip of her nose as she pouted. "Okay, so I need to do penance, right?"

She glared at him. "Possibly."

He took her mouth in a hard, fast kiss. "I know just the thing." He wasn't giving her the option of saying no. Not this time. He was taking her back to her room and marking her before the end of the night. "Let's go, Sarah."

"No. Gabe." She tugged on his hand. "Not yet."

He gritted his teeth, but the panic on her face held him back. "What more do you need, Sarah?" He gripped her shoulders before running his fingers through her hair. "Tell me, baby."

Her mouth opened but before she could reply his phone rang. He pulled it free from its holster and answered without looking. "Hello?"

"Gabe?"

He closed his eyes and tried to ignore the hurt in Sarah's eyes. If he'd looked at the fucking caller ID he would have let it go to voice mail but it was too late now. "Yeah, Chloe?"

"Look, I know you're probably busy with Sarah but do you think she'd mind if I borrowed you for a little while?"

He knew that tone in Chloe's voice. Something had happened, and his friendly little vixen was feeling down. "I'm not sure. What's the problem?" He kept his stare on Sarah, knowing she could hear everything Chloe said.

Not that it appeared to matter. The moment he asked what the problem was Sarah made a face and backed up a step. "See you later, Gabe."

He grabbed her wrist, holding tight when she tried to pull away. "Oh no, you're not going anywhere."

"Gabe? Crap, she's upset, isn't she? Have you marked her yet?"

Sarah stopped tugging. She glared up at Gabe. "What did she just say?"

He winced. "She's..." He took the phone away from his ear. "Look, baby, it's complicated."

"I'll say. Your girlfriend just called to ask you if you'd marked your mate yet."

He got right in her face, absurdly proud of the fact that she didn't back away from him. And how fucked up was that? "She's not my girlfriend, Sarah." There went that fucking eyebrow again. "Stop that."

"Stop what?"

"Stop doubting me, damn it."

"Stop giving me reasons to!" She yanked her wrist free and began walking off.

He didn't even hesitate. "Chloe? Sorry, you're on your own." He closed his phone and put it away, striding after Sarah as quickly as he could. "Sarah!"

She flipped him off and kept walking. From the way she was stomping he was pretty sure she was either picturing his or Chloe's face.

"Sarah!" He finally caught up to her and grabbed her arm.

An elbow jammed him hard in the stomach, knocking the wind out of him. Her foot stomped on his, earning her a surprised yowl. But what really got him was when she pulled away, spun and tried to kick him in the balls. He barely got his thigh in the way in time to stop some serious pain. "Jesus Christ, Sarah!"

She got into his face and put her finger dangerously close to his mouth. "You stay away from me, Gabriel Anderson. You hear me? I never want to see you again!"

That's it. There was only one way he was going to be able to get through to her, and Gabe knew it.

He pulled her tight, refusing to let her go, and finally,

finally marked her as his. Her knees buckled, but he didn't mind. There was no way he was letting her go. The scent of her orgasm rolled over him, soothing both him and his Puma, the knowledge that she belonged to him nearly triggering his own orgasm. He thrust a thigh between her legs, giving her something to ride as her pleasure continued to wash over her. His Puma longed to scream its triumph as his incredible mate finally relaxed in his arms. He purred against Sarah's neck, the urge to mount her right then and there so strong he barely resisted it.

"Get a room!"

Gabe lifted his head to see two kids, barely high school age, grinning at them. *The little shits.*

"Oh God."

He turned his head to see Sarah, wide-eyed, staring at the kids. They weren't Puma, and from their scent they weren't from Halle, but he could understand why she was freaked out. She buried her face against his chest. "I'm going to kill you."

He pulled his leg out from between hers, his cheeks flushing as some other kids laughed and clapped. One smart-ass actually held up a Hollywood Studios map with the number "7.5" written on it. "I might let you."

Chapter Eight

The door shut behind them with a final-sounding click. Sarah refused to turn around and face her mate. "So."

Silence.

She licked her lips nervously, knowing what was about to happen. It was sort of like worrying about the drippy faucet right after the dam had broken. "Want to watch a movie?"

"Sarah."

She shivered at the tone of voice. *Oh, boy.* Her lashes lowered before she'd even had time to think. Her dominant lover was in the room, and he would brook no refusal tonight. The emotion pouring off Gabe only sent her own arousal soaring.

"Come here."

She turned, studying him from underneath her lashes, one brow raised in challenge. As much as she wanted to belong to him, this was not the way she'd wanted things to go down. She needed something from him she still wasn't certain he could give her. Her own emotions were conflicting with his, the harmony she'd sensed in the other pairs of mates lacking in them.

He stood there, just watching her, those dark blue eyes of his slowly bleeding to gold. The sight was highly erotic, evidence of his desire for her.

Through an act of will she kept her own eyes brown, knowing it would spur him on. His nostrils flared and she knew he could smell her arousal. He held out his hand, palm up, and waited. Patient as a cat.

Her mouth curled as she watched him stand there. *Damn.* Knowing him he would stand there all day, too. *Stubborn son of a bitch.*

And wasn't that the main source of their problems? He'd been too stubborn to just *ask* her, about anything. And here he was, holding out his hand...

Wait. He's just standing there, holding out his hand.

He *was* asking her. He was asking for her compliance, for her to bend her will to his, if only here in the bedroom. For the most part he'd treated her as an equal out of bed.

Like a man treated his mate.

Was it enough that he asked, even if it wasn't verbal? She studied him, reliving every moment of the last two days. Every hour of their lovemaking sifted through her mind. The times she'd had to listen to Chloe talk about her time with Gabe was still a shaft of pain she couldn't deny. Yet here he stood, in her room, having marked her *in public* (and God would she ever get over *that?*) holding out his hand and waiting. For her.

She took a deep breath and let go of the shield she'd held in front of her senses. It was harder than she'd thought it would be, but she pulled it down bit by bit until she could feel everything he felt.

And it damn near dropped her to her knees. For the first time she fully understood the need, yes the *love* in him without her own doubts and insecurities clouding her senses, and it was *glorious.*

All of her earlier posturing was gone as she allowed herself to bend to his will. The arousal moved through her, slow as honey and just as sweet. She moved to take his hand, the thought of his fangs sinking into her, of him marking her again and claiming her for his own almost enough to bring her to her knees.

When their hands met, his face lit with savage joy. He didn't give her the slightest chance to push him away. Pulling her to him he bit into her shoulder, sending her into a screaming orgasm that was part pain, all pleasure. He held her tight, thrusting his thigh in between her legs, allowing her to ride it as the dark waves rolled over her, the emotions pouring off him throwing her higher than she'd ever been.

Without even thinking about it her Puma struck, marking Gabe, pulling a groaning shudder from him. He held her head in place as her teeth slid into him, his hands tangling in her hair and tugging on her. "That's it, baby." He used his free hand to begin slowly shredding her tank top, the tips of his claws leaving delicious trails of fire in their wake. The need in him spiked, savage and brutal and aimed only at her. They began walking backwards towards the bed. He took his hand out of her hair to pick her up by her ass, her feet dangling from the floor. She took her fangs out of his neck and held on.

"Wrap your legs around my waist."

She complied just as he tipped her backwards, her shoulders landing on the bed. Her ass was in midair, her hands clutching the bedspread to keep from falling.

"Good girl." His fingers moved to the button of her shorts, undoing them and the zipper swiftly. "You're going to trust me. Understand?"

She licked her lips and nodded.

"Say it."

"I trust you, sir."

One large hand went to the small of her back as the other

one started to slide her shorts off. He grunted as they slid down and he realized she hadn't worn any panties.

He took the shorts to the tops of her knees before his hand went to his own shorts. He wrestled them down, exposing the long, hard line of his cock. "I owe you, baby."

Her eyes widened, her ass cheeks clenching in anticipation at the determination on his face. His hand stroked her ass, clutching one cheek before moving to the other one. "I'm going to redden this pretty ass of yours."

She bit back her whimper.

"Up on the bed, hands and knees."

She scrambled, awkward with her shorts around her knees, but she knew better than to take them off. She knew him well enough to know that the sight of them was a turn-on for him. She bent down, shoulders to the bed, ass cheeks stuck up in the air, and waited for his hand.

She didn't have to wait long. She felt the sting immediately as he swatted her. "Count."

"One. Two. Three." She felt the cheeks of her ass begin to burn, her pussy clenching in anticipation of the next blow. She still didn't know what it was that made her crave this, but no way was she about to complain.

"I'm going to fuck this ass." Another swat landed, her whimper escaping before she could bite it back. It felt like her butt was on fire. He stroked the red globes, his hand soothing on the sensitive skin. "You'll look so pretty with my cock sliding between these red cheeks."

Her clit throbbed at the thought of feeling him there. They'd done it once before in the dreams, and the sensations had been wild beyond belief. "Please, sir."

"Please what?"

"Please fuck me."

She felt him move back on the bed. "Not quite yet." She closed her eyes as his hands slid to her hips. "First I want to admire my ass."

"Get a mirror," she muttered.

Another slap had her squealing. "What was that?"

The amusement in his voice had her relaxing back against his hand. "Nothing. Sir."

His teeth nipped her hip. "Are you sure? It sounded like you had something to say."

If you don't fuck me soon I'm going to kill you. She had the feeling if she told him that she would wind up staying there, ass in the air, while he went and did something else. "I said you have a very fine ass, sir."

He laughed as he stroked hers. "That I do."

The first swipe of his wet, warm tongue took her by surprise and she jumped. "Tasty, too." Gabe's tongue rolled around the globes of her ass, occasionally dipping in between the cleft of her cheeks to swipe at her pussy.

The sudden feel of his teeth on her ass sent her spinning once more into orgasm. She drummed her feet against the mattress, grateful his hands had become firm on her hips, keeping her from falling.

She didn't realize until she came down off the high that he'd marked her ass.

"Mine."

The smug tone of his voice had her looking over her shoulder.

He was staring down at the mark he'd put on her with so much male satisfaction she rolled her eyes.

The satisfaction leeched from his face, a frown forming

between his eyes. "Damn. I'm going to have to save fucking my ass for another day."

"Why?" *Well, don't I just sound needy?* The whine in her voice had her mentally wincing.

"I don't have lube."

Okay, the thought of that really did have her wincing. She clenched her ass cheeks, her ankles crossing in protest.

"I gather going in with just spit for lube isn't your idea of fun?" He grinned when she glared at him, sliding his cock up and down the crease of her pussy. "I guess we'll have to do something else, then."

He rammed home, shoving her forward on the bed, and began pounding into her. The fact that her legs were together made the sensations that much tighter. His hands landed on either side of her head, his thighs slapping against the heated flesh of her ass. She could feel his balls banging against her engorged clit as he fucked her without mercy.

He nipped the nape of her neck, his teeth grazing the sensitive skin, her Puma purring its approval at her mate's show of dominance. She moved against him, fucking him back, reveling in the feel of him shuttling in and out of her body.

I wonder...

Sarah opened up her senses, felt for Gabe, and *pushed.* Every emotion she was experiencing poured out of her and into him. Gabe choked, his hips stopping. Sarah whimpered and he echoed it. The sensation when he began to move again rocketed through them.

She could feel it, the connection between them. She knew he was experiencing everything he was doing to her. The exquisite pleasure was blinding, building up and up. They fed off each other's pending orgasm, the waves crashing through them both. They wanted. They *needed.* She was gasping, begging for more, his low growls pushing at her. Before she could voice the need his hands were on her ass, smacking her, gently, harshly, alternating pats with slaps, inching her closer and closer to an explosion that just might kill her. His teeth clamped down on her shoulder again, pinning her in place and sending her into her third orgasm. She screamed breathlessly, pulsing around the hard flesh that continued to batter into her, her mind and heart shattering along with her body.

She began begging, pleading with him to move faster, harder, the pleasure rolling on and on until she thought she might black out. Her claws shredded the bedspread uncontrollably as she felt the beginnings of *his* orgasm rip through him, the sensations shoving her into a fourth orgasm so hard she saw stars.

"Fuck, fuck!" His head whipped up, his Puma screaming as he emptied himself into her body. The fact that he'd lost enough control that his Puma nearly came out was an immense source of satisfaction to her. Gabe rarely lost control.

He collapsed to the side, pulling her down with him, curling around her body as they both struggled for breath. His cock twitched inside her, his arm around her waist preventing her from pulling away. "No. Stay where you are."

She had the feeling the drugged-sounding command wasn't just about her body.

She settled down against her mate, loving the feel of his flesh inside her, the little flash of panic he'd felt smoothing out into a contented rumble. Little nibbling kisses against the back of her neck soothed her. With a small smile she allowed herself to drift peacefully, secure in the knowledge that her mate would keep her safe. Hell, she even allowed herself to purr.

Take that, Chloe's of the world. Gabe is mine.

"What's that smug look for?"

She smiled, the feel of her lips curving tickling his skin. "I'm not sure I should answer that."

He turned her, wanting to see her face. It was important that he see her face now, almost as important as the feel of her in his mind. He'd never experienced anything like what she'd done to him. She'd more than mated him, she *owned* him now, in ways he wasn't certain he understood. "Do you believe me now?"

"About what?"

He grimaced. "Chloe."

She bit her lip.

Gabe sighed. *Obviously not.* "Why is it you still feel I have something going with Chloe?"

She winced. "I don't, not really."

"But something is still bothering you. What is it?"

"The bracelet."

Ah. He'd wondered when they'd get around to that. "Yes, I gave her a bracelet. She's a friend; someone who I thought was doing me a favor. I swear to you, nothing has ever happened between us. *Nothing.* It would be like having sex with my kid sister."

"You don't have a kid sister."

He growled. "You know what I mean." He tipped her chin up. "Believe me. You can ask her if you like. She already knows who her mate is, and it isn't me. She's just trying to figure out how to claim him."

"Who?" Her eyes went wide. "Jim really *is* her mate?"

He nodded, choosing to ignore the fact that she'd suspected as much. There'd been enough grief between them over Jim and Chloe. "She volunteers as a vet's assistant while she's earning

211

her doctorate in veterinary medicine, so they're together constantly. She says he turned her down, told her she's too young for him."

She made a face. "He did. And I called him on it, too, but he's stuck in the belief that she's not mature enough for him or something like that."

He caressed that beautiful face, dragging his thumb over her lips just to feel her smile. "Whenever I talked to her we discussed mostly you and Jim. Now do you believe me?"

She stroked his chest, relaxing against him with a nod. "Okay. I believe you."

He pressed a kiss to her forehead, hoping he'd finally laid her fears to rest. "I love you, Sarah." He opened his heart, hoping that she'd finally *feel* it.

When she gave him that mysterious, feminine little smile, his heart nearly exploded from happiness. "I know."

He bent to her, determined to drink from that happiness and never let it go.

It was two-thirty in the morning, but Gabe couldn't sleep. He breathed in deep, the scent of his mate surrounding him. Her salty skin was under his tongue. Her heated ass nestled against his groin. And she'd trusted him enough to fall asleep.

Or at least he hoped it was trust, and not sleepy fucked-out exhaustion. *Well, okay, I could live with fucked-out exhaustion.* He smirked, listening to her even breathing.

It was a heady feeling, holding her in his arms while awake. What was even headier was the knowledge that, even though she could take him down with a thought, render him helpless and begging and crying like a wimp, she'd allowed him to dominate her. And he wasn't going to even try and fool himself on that one, either. If she'd wished to she could have stopped him cold at any point. His mate was a lot stronger than he'd dared give her credit for. Just one day of watching her with Jim had proven it beyond a doubt.

If he'd had to go through *months* of that, he'd have wound up insane, or a murderer. Or both. The sex they'd had earlier just cemented it. She'd taken him, pulled him into her, held tight and given him the ride of his fucking life.

Thank God she hadn't given up on him. Because she could have. She had the strength to walk away and never looked back. And it would have been his own God damn fault for listening to the fucking Bear instead of his own instincts.

He shuddered at the thought of living without Sarah. What had he been thinking, holding off on the mating? He'd been so busy protecting her from their separation that he'd failed to see what it would do to her.

In the end he'd nearly destroyed them both, and for what?

Well, he was determined now that Sarah would never have any doubts about *exactly* how much he wanted her. *Needed* her.

He knew that, at certain times, he'd have to bow down to her. She was the Omega. He was merely the Marshall's Second. He rolled over onto his back, pulling the covers over them both before settling down, arms over his head. He stared at the ceiling, trying to determine exactly how he felt about that. The more he thought about it, the more the lack of anxiety was a relief. He'd have no problems with it. He might be the dominant partner in their physical relationship but when it came to the Pride she outranked him. If needed, he would bow down happily, knowing his baby would be back in his bed and begging for him, if she didn't have him begging first.

He couldn't keep the grin off his face. He didn't want a doormat for a spouse, and Fate had seen to it he hadn't gotten one. Sarah had proven to him, and to herself, that she was strong enough to hold him off, but also strong enough to let herself go for him.

He blinked. *Damn.* He tried to hold back his groan but some slipped past. He'd forgotten to give her the ring he'd bought for her for Christmas. He'd have to give it to her first thing in the morning. Maybe he'd take her to France in Epcot for breakfast and feed her beignets before asking her to marry him. He hoped she liked the simple, square-cut diamond set in yellow gold he'd gotten her.

He closed his eyes and allowed sleep to wash over him. He wasn't surprised when he met Sarah in his dream.

She was everything he ever wanted to dream of, and more.

Epilogue

Emma was pacing behind the curtain, her lip between her teeth, her brown eyes wild. "Are you *sure* I look all right?"

Sarah squelched the urge to use her powers to soothe Emma. Right then the bride-to-be was so dense with anxiety that anything Sarah threw at her would just bounce off unless Sarah really exerted herself. Sarah was still so new at this she was afraid she'd make Emma too relaxed and the Curana would have to be *carried* down the aisle. "You look great, Emma."

"Trust me. You look wonderful." Sheri hugged Emma, careful of the Curana's carefully arranged hair.

"Thanks. I think." Emma bit her lip. "Where's Becky?"

"She went to use the litter box." Belle grinned, leaning against the wall. Sarah was pretty sure Belle's hip was bothering her but the Luna had refused to use her cane, saying it clashed with her outfit.

Sarah was also pretty sure Rick would have something to say about that later, when the two of them were alone. He'd already been back twice to check on Belle, earning a snarl from his Luna. She'd muttered something about an air horn, but Rick hadn't seemed intimidated in the least.

Becky was just coming back from her trip to the ladies' room when Emma's very human wedding planner bustled in. "All right, ladies, it's almost time. Is everyone ready?"

Emma gulped. "Yes." She breathed in deep, then blew it out again. "I'm fine."

She wasn't, but Sarah wasn't about to say anything. Emma was practically vibrating with anxiety.

Emma's father came into the room, his salt-and-pepper hair gleaming. "You look wonderful, sweetheart." He placed a soft kiss on his daughter's cheeks, his eyes shining with pride. It was easy to see where Emma got her looks from. "Your mother wanted me to tell you that Max looks very handsome."

Emma visibly relaxed, the sensation sweeping into Sarah, nearly knocking her off her feet. Emma felt everything so intensely it constantly threw Sarah for a loop. "Really?"

"Really." He put Emma's arm through his own and turned to the wedding planner. "Are we ready?"

The music swelled, the planner shushing them all and lining them up. Sarah watched as the wedding planner counted down. "Now," the woman hissed, shooing Sarah down the aisle.

She walked, holding her small bouquet of ivory calla lilies in front of her. Her fuchsia-colored gown swished around her ankles, the simple shape a perfect match for Emma's more non-traditional gown. She had to admit the color looked stunning, and the simple strapless A-line dress was perfect for all of their shapes and sizes.

She took her place in the gazebo in front of the altar, her eyes automatically drifting past all of the other men to her man. Gabe looked incredibly hot in his black tux and dark gold vest. He blew her a kiss, smiling at her when she blushed.

Next came Belle, the blonde Luna making her stately way down the aisle. Rick damn near growled at the sight of her limping, but he remained in place behind Max and Simon, earning himself a sweet smile.

Sheri glided out, the fuchsia of her dress startling against her alabaster skin and white blonde hair. Her sensitive eyes were covered by her white sunglasses. A soft smile graced her lips as she took her place in front of Belle.

Becky stepped out from behind the curtain, her wild curls tamed into a sleek fall of light brown hair that reached down to her waist. One white calla lily was tucked behind her ear. She smiled at Simon and winked before taking her place as maid of honor. Sarah turned to find Simon staring at Becky with something akin to adoration.

The music changed and Sarah turned. She heard the gasps of the guests and smiled, her eyes darting to see the stunned look on Max's face.

The Curana looked like a queen in her gown. Strapless, simple, the embroidered, bold stripe of color at the neckline of the dress drew back into a long colored and embroidered train the same color as the bridesmaids' dresses. An enlarged version of the embroidered band circled the bottom of the dress. The rest of the dress was ivory, as was the embroidery itself. A small gold and citrine tiara rested on top of curled hair that had been styled half up, half down, one dark curl resting on her creamy shoulder. Her jewelry was a simple necklace of gold and citrines with matching earrings. Her bouquet was a more elaborate version of her bridesmaids', the color matching their dresses. Her father walked proudly beside her, a king giving away his princess.

"Holy fuck." Max winced when Reverend Glaston reached out and smacked him gently upside the head, much to the amusement of the guests. Emma merely winked, her expression full of laughter.

The rest of the wedding went off without a hitch, both Max and Emma expressing their love for each other in clear voices, but Sarah barely heard it. Her gaze was drawn again and again to her mate, not surprised to find his never left her. She had to resist the urge to play with the diamond engagement ring he'd given her a few days before. He hadn't given her a chance to say no. She'd woken up to find it already on her finger, his purring contentment humming through her. She'd been wearing it ever since.

"I now pronounce you husband and wife."

Sarah blinked and turned back to the ceremony to find Max tugging Emma into his arms.

"Max, wait for me to say it first, please." The reverend was looking over his glasses at Max, who just grinned and shrugged. "Max?"

"Hmm?" Max was staring down into the glowing eyes of his mate.

The reverend nodded. "You may kiss the bride."

Max bent down and kissed Emma reverently.

Sarah felt tears start up, the beauty of the moment, the love of the Pride and the newly married couple so full and sweet she couldn't contain it.

But over it all, she felt the love of her mate, her Gabriel, and all was right again. She blew him a kiss, not surprised when his eyes sparkled with gold.

Yup, all was right with her world.

The reception was a blast. Max and Emma had chosen Cinderella's Castle Courtyard for the reception, a classy, elegant venue with a dash of fun that matched them to a T. The only dark spot was a small fight between Chloe and Jim, but only a soft, whispered word in Jim's ear had been needed to stop the fight from going much further.

Strangely enough, the Pride seemed much more accepting

of Belle now that she was no longer a member. Marie Howard even shook Belle's hand, something Sarah would never have expected, although the lingering distaste Sarah could sense was carefully hidden behind Marie's social mask. Belle accepted the gesture graciously, but Sarah knew the Luna would never trust Marie again.

Sarah stood in the shadows, watching Chloe dance with a dark-haired man, and sighed. She was going to have to get used to that sight. Gabe might have explained that Chloe was no more than a friend to him, but it would take time before she was completely over the feelings she got when she saw the two of them together. Oh, she trusted Gabe. His love surrounded her constantly, as if he was consciously wrapping her up in it, never allowing her to forget who she belonged to. Still, it hurt deep inside to watch them together, despite all of Gabe's reassurances. She had the feeling that only time, and a steady diet of Gabe's brand of loving, would make those sensations go away completely.

And one thing she could think of to do to help that along was to see to it that Jim and Chloe got together. Maybe watching the Fox claim her reluctant mate would finally bury the jealousy she felt towards her once and for all.

"Hey."

Sarah turned to smile up at Rick, surprised the Wolf had sought her out. It wasn't that she and Rick hadn't spoken before. She'd actually done what she could to make sure he knew how bad things had gotten for Belle before he whisked her off to the Poconos. She gave him a silly, exaggerated bow. "Your Alphaness."

He snorted. "Cute." He nodded towards Gabe and Chloe. "You have nothing to worry about, you know."

Sarah stared at him, shocked. "Um, okay?"

His lips twisted. "He's not into Chloe that way." His entire face relaxed as his gaze came to rest on Belle. "He looks at you the way I look at Belle." Rick grinned down at Sarah. "Trust me, the only thing on his mind right now is how quickly he can get you back to your room and get you naked."

Sarah blushed. "Are you sure about that?"

"More sure than I want to be, trust me." He took a sip of his wine with a grimace. "I...can hear him."

Sarah blinked. "You mean...?"

Rick nodded. "Not sure what exactly that means, but yeah."

Sarah was fascinated. Belle had told her about Rick's psychic connection with the rest of his Pack. She never thought it could extend outside of it. "Can you hear anyone else?"

"You, Sheri, Adrian, Max, Emma, Becky, Simon... Do you people think of anything other than fucking, by the way? And they call *us* dogs."

Sarah nearly choked on her wine. "What about the rest of the Pride?"

He frowned. She could just about feel the force of his thoughts roaming the party. "Faintly, but they're there. If I was far enough away I doubt I'd hear them at all."

"Do you think it has something to do with Belle?"

All of that energy suddenly focused on the Luna, who tossed a sultry look over her shoulder at the Alpha Wolf before returning to her conversation with Emma. "More than likely. She's the first Puma Luna, after all. For all I know our kids will be Wolves with retractable claws."

"And amazing psychic powers?"

Rick shrugged. "If it's meant to be." He grinned at something he saw over Sarah's much-shorter head. "I'll see you later, Omega."

"Later, Wolfman."

He huffed a laugh, shaking his head as he wandered off.

Sarah looked up, startled at the fireworks suddenly going off overhead. She wasn't the least surprised when strong arms circled her waist. Soft lips brushed against her neck, the prickles of her mate's five o'clock shadow sending delicious shivers down her spine. And in the darkness and the magic, Gabe claimed her again, his teeth sliding beneath her skin and marking her for everyone to see, in or out of dreams.

About the Author

Dana Marie Bell wrote her first short story when she was thirteen years old. She attended the High School for Creative and Performing Arts for creative writing, where freedom of expression was the order of the day. When her parents moved out of the city and placed her in a Catholic high school for her senior year she tried desperately to get away, but the nuns held fast, and she graduated with honors despite herself.

Dana has lived primarily in the Northeast (Pennsylvania, New Jersey and Delaware, to be precise), with a brief stint on the US Virgin Island of St. Croix. She lives with her soul-mate and husband Dusty, their two maniacal children, an evil ice-cream stealing cat and a bull terrier that thinks it's a Pekinese.

You can learn more about Dana at:

www.danamariebell.com

GREAT
CHEAP
FUN

Discover eBooks!

THE FASTEST WAY TO GET THE HOTTEST NAMES

Get your favorite authors on your favorite reader, long before they're out in print! Ebooks from Samhain go wherever you go, and work with whatever you carry—Palm, PDF, Mobi, and more.

Samhain Publishing ltd

WWW.SAMHAINPUBLISHING.COM

LaVergne, TN USA
29 August 2010
195058LV00009B/2/P